A TIME
FOR
LOVE

A TIME
FOR
LOVE

•

JOYE AMES

AVALON BOOKS
NEW YORK

PRINTED IN THE UNITED STATES OF AMERICA
ON ACID-FREE PAPER
BY HADDON CRAFTSMEN, BLOOMSBURG, PENNSYLVANIA

For Henry Koch, Chicago Fire Department,
who never finished school but taught an
eager young writer to value her work.
Thanks, Grampa.

Chapter One

The smoke was too thick to be able to see clearly, but Officer Annie O'Malley fought her way through it. She might not be able to see, but she could hear. Somewhere in that smoke-filled warehouse, a baby was trapped. She could hear its feeble crying. She'd seen weirder things in her five years on the force but none more pitiful.

She kept her body close to the damp cement floor and listened, trying not to cough and splutter so much that she couldn't hear the baby. She'd tied her partner's wet handkerchief over her nose and mouth to act as a filter for the black smoke but it wasn't much help.

If she could see something besides the light reflected back to her from her flashlight beam!

The warehouse floor looked empty. Not even a rat in sight. Yet still she heard the baby. The cries were becoming weaker.

She coughed, tried to clear her throat, and squinted her eyes against the terrible smoke.

If only it were an older child so that she could call to it and get a better fix. She could reassure the child and explain that she was trying to find him or her. She had plenty of experience with older children in trouble. But a baby . . .

Then she saw a shape in the middle of the floor. The street light shining through the rotted wood that was supposed to cover the window acted like a halo on the fragile carrier.

Annie crawled on her hands and knees, trying to stay away from the worst of the heat and smoke. The baby in the carrier was silent and unmoving in the flashlight beam.

Please, she prayed silently, please let it be alive.

Tears streaming from her eyes, nearly blinded by the smoke, she reached the infant carrier's side. She could see that the blanket was sooty with the heavy smoke. The baby was wearing a frilly little dress and had a bow in her curly dark hair.

A little girl. Annie coughed convulsively and put down the flashlight. She put her hand to the baby's chest and was relieved to feel the little body still moving.

At her touch, the baby cried fitfully and flayed her little arms uselessly against the smoke that was rapidly filling her lungs. Annie tried to quiet her, although, she reasoned, it was probably a good thing that she was crying. It would keep her little lungs clear.

She picked up the baby with the dirty blanket and unzipped her heavy jacket, tucking the child inside, next to her heart. There was a note pinned to the top of the carrier and she took it as well. It might give some clue to the baby's identity.

Little pieces of fiery wood had begun to fall from the high ceiling to the floor. They illuminated the place eerily, and made Annie's efforts to escape the warehouse even more dangerous. If one of those pieces fell on her, she could be knocked unconscious or even have her clothing ignite.

"Don't go into a burning building!" she remembered her police academy trainer saying again and again. "That's why we have the fire department. Let them handle the fires."

She hadn't wanted to run into a burning building. But when she and her partner had arrived on the scene, the fire hadn't been reported. That meant it would be at least ten minutes until the fire truck arrived and that would be without a traffic tie-up.

She'd heard the baby when she'd opened the warehouse door. She and Tom had looked at one another.

"The trucks will be here in a few minutes," he'd assured her. "Let's not panic."

Annie had looked at the angry red fire already sparking through the upper story windows and the roof. It burned like the sun against the evening sky.

"That baby doesn't have a few minutes," she'd told her partner. "I'm going in."

"Annie . . ." he'd begun, then held his peace. He'd been her partner for too long not to know that she was headstrong and sometimes a little prone to take action when he thought it might be better to wait.

She was a good cop, he considered, taking her baton and giving her his handkerchief after he'd dampened it in some rainwater from the drain spout.

"Be careful," he warned. "Cap will kill me if anything stupid happens to you."

Annie smiled and tied the handkerchief across her nose and mouth. Her father, Mike O'Malley, was a captain in another squad. If he'd seen her about to enter a burning building without a firefighter, he would have knocked her silly.

The baby was squirming fitfully inside her zipped jacket. The handkerchief was dry on her face. It was harder to see in the warehouse, even though she was barely above floor level. She kept looking for the light from the open doorway but she couldn't find it.

"Don't panic," she whispered to herself. "Keep going. You're headed in the right direction."

Too many times she'd heard stories about how people panicked in fires and got turned around. She had to keep going the way she thought she'd come into the building.

Her chest hurt from the smoke and the effort to breathe through it. It was getting hot in the building even next to the cold floor. She didn't want to look up, knowing the roof could be about to collapse. As it was, her back itched with the fear that a burning chunk of the warehouse was about to hit her.

She kept going, glad to feel that the baby was still moving and making small, pitiful noises. She was protected a little from the smoke and heat in her jacket. Hopefully, there wasn't much damage done to her lungs from the smoke.

Who could have done such a stupid thing? she wondered, trying to keep her mind occupied with anything but the fire while she crawled to what she hoped was safety.

The way the baby girl had been put in the carrier, dressed up and with a note attached, smacked of abandonment.

But surely the fire was an accident. The mother or father may have left her there but hadn't known that there would be a fire. The warehouse had been abandoned for years.

She coughed, trying to find a small space of breathable air, but there didn't seem to be any left. She ripped the handkerchief from her face and wheezed in some soot, coughing and shaking with the effort to keep going.

Surely she should have reached that stupid door by then, she decided angrily, turning on her back to rest for just a moment. She reached a hand into her jacket to comfort the baby, who was making tiny mewling sounds.

Her skin was so soft, and a little downy, like velvet. She was very thin, not like her sister's baby, who was chubby cheeked and had legs like a linebacker.

Anne sighed, finding it easier to breathe with her back against the cold floor. The baby was quiet as well, and she thought that it was probably better to wait there for a few minutes. Help would be coming.

Sparks flew around them and small fire devils leaped from rotted timber to old debris, igniting everything they touched. They looked like stars or comets streaking across the night sky that was the collapsing warehouse roof.

She had to get out of there, she reminded herself, trying to pull herself out of her oxygen-deprived stupor.

She turned over and started to crawl again, but her knees buckled under her and her last thought was for the baby she carried against her chest, cradling the small body with her arms.

That was how firefighter Tony Rousso found her a few minutes later. Breathing clean air behind a mask, covered with protective gear, he stooped to lift her from her fetal position on the floor.

He couldn't believe it when his company had arrived on the scene of the warehouse fire and found that an officer had already entered the building.

Was she a moron? he wondered, kicking in what little remained of the wooden door at the entrance. Or did she just have a death wish?

Her partner had told them that she'd heard a baby inside and had gone in to investigate. She should have been back out by then. Unless she was in trouble.

Tony wasn't sure if he admired her partner's position at the door doing his duty or if he wondered at the man's lack of courage for not risking it to find out what had happened to his partner. It was one thing to do your duty. Loyalty was something of even greater worth.

He wouldn't have wanted to think that his partner would have thought the regulations were so important that he would have let him die.

Tony lifted the woman easily in his arms, not bothering to position her in the fireman's cradle. She'd been going in the right direction and had been only a few yards from the door.

How many times had he found someone trapped in a burning building just a few feet from safety? How many nightmares had plagued him where he'd seen their faces? It was part of his job, just like the good rescues.

The woman moved when he lifted her—a good sign. Something else moved inside her jacket, making small noises that didn't identify it as human. It could have been a dog or a cat for all he could tell. The officer had managed to rescue whatever it was, despite breaking the rules. He had to admire her for that courage.

He ran out the door with her in his arms, held tightly against his chest. The fire demons raced across what was left of the roof. As he reached the clean night air, the ceiling collapsed to the basement of the warehouse.

Tony laid the officer on a blanket on the ground and called for oxygen. The paramedics hadn't arrived yet. He was on his own while his comrades fought the fire that raged a few hundred feet from them.

He improvised, giving the officer oxygen from his own breathing gear. Another abandonment of the regulations. It seemed to be the night for it. She was unconscious and filthy with smoke, but she looked vaguely familiar. She'd lost her cap somewhere inside the building. She was lucky to be alive.

He unzipped her jacket and the squirming thing within it came to life, crying loudly and reaching her arms out to him.

The baby was covered in black soot. Her little dress was torn and filthy. But she was alive, and if her crying was any indication, she was going to be all right.

He borrowed an oxygen mask from another firefighter and used it on the baby the best he could. She didn't want to be covered with the huge mask and fought him with her tiny arms and legs to keep it away from her.

The little girl would have died without the officer's intervention, he realized, hoping they both recovered. They would never have been able to reach her in time to save her from the ceiling collapse.

What had she been doing in there? he wondered, trying to keep the masks on both of his patients. There were no homes near the warehouse. Only miles of the worst commercial property, most of it abandoned like the warehouse.

Even if someone had chosen to abandon the baby, he couldn't believe they didn't mean her to be found and given a new home. There was no way for anyone to have known about the fire.

The officer started to cough and moved uneasily on the coarse blanket, opening her eyes and staring up at him with a mixture of relief and surprise.

"The baby," she said quickly, putting her hand to her jacket.

"She's okay," Tony reassured her. "Paramedics are on the way."

Flashing lights and blaring sirens followed his pronouncement. The noise from the fire roared across the shouts of the firefighters trying to stop it from spreading.

"I know you," the officer said in a rasping voice, her throat irritated with smoke and heat. "You're Rousso, aren't you?"

He looked at her more closely. The matted hair was copper bright beneath the soot from the fire. Her eyes were startlingly blue and her mouth . . .

"O'Malley," he recalled. "I thought I recognized you."

Annie frowned. She didn't know how happy he would be to recognize her. They saw each other from time to time but didn't usually speak. He'd asked her out once while she'd been dating Sean. She'd turned him down. Maybe a little nastily. She'd been having trouble with Sean that day.

"That was a stupid thing you did running in there without gear or oxygen."

"I know," she admitted, glancing down at her soot-streaked uniform. "I did what I thought was right."

She struggled to sit up while the paramedics attended the baby on the other side of her. Tony watched her, then grabbed her arm and helped her up.

"Don't worry, I'm not writing you up for it. But you owe me," he responded, crouching down close beside her.

"Oh?" she asked, wondering if he knew that she and Sean weren't together anymore.

Was he going to ask her out again? Word traveled through the departments. Especially if someone was interested.

"The next time you want to run into a burning building, don't do it. You came this close to being in there when that roof collapsed."

"Oh." So much for that, she thought, feeling foolish. Just because he'd asked her out once didn't mean it would ever happen again. He was probably married anyway.

"But you did get the baby out," he relented, seeing the disappointment on her black-streaked face. "And she seems to be all right."

"I'd like to know what she was doing in there." Annie rapidly changed the subject. "If she was abandoned, it was a stupid place to do it."

Tony shrugged. "Mother or father could have put her in there, then set the fire."

"That's horrible!"

"I'm sure you've heard worse, coming from a police family."

She glanced up at him. "That doesn't make it okay."

"I didn't say it did," he shot back. "We'll know later if the fire was set or not."

"Officer," the paramedic nearest her, called to her. "Do you need help?"

"I'm fine," she answered, despite a headache and a raw throat.

"She was out cold for a full ten minutes," Tony replied, interrupting with a shake of his dark head. "Sorry, O'Malley. We've both broken enough rules for one night."

"I'm fine," she reiterated with a grimace. "I don't need to go with them."

"You need some oxygen," he answered firmly. "I imagine your throat is pretty sore."

"A little," she answered honestly. "But not enough to ride down to the hospital and fill out the paperwork on an injury."

"You can hold the baby," the paramedic told her. He smiled at Rousso. "That always gets 'em."

"So, you're going to the hospital?" Tom asked awkwardly. He watched the gathering crowd with one eye while he spoke with his partner. "Need a ride home?"

"I'll grab a taxi," she said. "Thanks, Tom. See you tomorrow."

She stood up, swaying a little when she reached her feet. Rousso put a quick hand under her arm to steady her.

"Okay, okay," she agreed, her body making his argument for him. "I'm going in with them."

"Hey!" Rousso walked with her to the ambulance behind the paramedic carrying the baby. "You're a hero! You saved a baby! You can't buy press like that."

She slanted her eyes at him. "Or a report like that! The captain is going to have my head."

Tony laughed. "I heard you had connections there. Isn't Mike O'Malley your father?"

"Yes," she said through clenched teeth. "And he's going to have my head too."

"Get cleaned up," he advised, helping her into the back of the ambulance. "Let them treat your throat and give you some oxygen. You'll feel better."

"Thanks," she began, looking back at him as she took a seat on the side of the vehicle and the paramedics closed the doors.

He waved, then turned away. She watched him put on his mask again and join the others still fighting the fire. The ambulance started its siren and pulled away. The orange light from the burning building became smaller and smaller against the night sky.

She'd wanted to thank Rousso for saving her life. It might be months before she saw him again. They had to be called to the same place, on the same shift.

Maybe she could write him a note or send him a card, she considered, watching as the paramedic fought with the baby to give her oxygen.

"She's not burned, is she?" Annie asked the man.

"Not as far as we can tell," he replied.

"I could hold her for you. Maybe calm her down," she volunteered.

"Sure," he agreed readily. "She's pretty tense."

Annie took the screaming baby in her arms. The little hands and feet kicked and the little face crumpled into a tight grimace as tears spilled down her sooty face.

She rocked the little girl close to her and hummed in her ear. The baby had to be exhausted, as well as frightened, she reasoned. She held her tightly. Gradually, the crying was a little less and the tiny, fragile body relaxed. She was fitful but calm, making it easier to keep the oxygen mask on her face.

Traffic was light on the roads that evening and they made excellent time to the hospital. Nurses took the baby from her as soon as the vehicle had stopped at the emergency entrance. Annie could hear the little girl crying again as they hustled her down the sterile halls but there was nothing else she could do to comfort her.

Regulations wouldn't be broken any further. The baby would be thoroughly examined, then a social worker would be assigned to her case and if there was a foster home available, she would be taken there until they could find one of her relatives or provide a more permanent home.

If there wasn't a home available, she would be left in the care of the hospital staff until further arrangements could be made.

It was cold and impersonal, but it was the only system for dealing with the thousands of abandoned babies and children they brought in every year. Annie always liked to think that they were going someplace better. Almost any place they were wanted had to be better.

She wrapped her empty arms around her waist and followed a nurse to an examining room.

She saw children and babies left abandoned, every day. Yet something about this baby bothered her more than most. She didn't know what it was; maybe she was just getting old. Five years on the force could do that to a person. Her father and her mother had warned her before she took the shield.

No, she reasoned, stripping off her filthy uniform and donning a green hospital gown with the awful tie strings on the back. She was tired and dirty. She needed a hot shower and some clean clothes. And a strong cup of coffee. Then she'd be fine again.

She was balanced. She was focused. She just wanted to hold that baby again!

Well, what did she expect? she considered silently, while she endured the doctor's prodding and poking. She was almost twenty-five years old. Just because she hadn't taken the time yet to have children didn't mean that she didn't want children.

She hadn't seriously considered another relationship since Sean had left her. There just didn't seem to be enough time with double shifts and community service projects. Then there was her family with their constant flow of weddings, funerals, and birthdays.

It was wonderful coming from a large family but it was time consuming. There was always something going on with the uncles, aunts, or cousins. Not to mention her own eight brothers and sisters.

She listened to women who complained about their biological clocks ticking, prodding them to have children. She wasn't old enough to feel that way. But holding that baby reminded her of her own childhood. It reminded her that there was another life besides just going to work and coming home to an empty apartment.

A baby was soft smiles and gentle sighs. She was a tiny person who needed care and kindness. She was someone to love in a world where love seemed to be too difficult to maintain.

Of course she knew that there would be problems. She'd watched her brothers and sisters with their own children. She'd taken care of plenty of her younger siblings when she was still at home. She knew the responsibility, but she also knew the rewards.

First, she reminded herself, she had to find the right man.

"Well, I think you're all right, Officer . . ." The doctor checked the chart before he proceeded, ". . . O'Malley. You were fortunate. The nurse will give you some throat spray for that raw throat but I think you're fit for duty otherwise."

"Thanks, Doctor," she responded, getting up from

the examination table. "There was a baby, a little girl brought in with me. Did you see her?"

He frowned. "Sure. She's okay too. A social worker was already in the room before I got there. She'll be fine."

"That's great. Thanks."

"Any leads on her parents?"

"Not as far as I know," she told him. "The baby was in a warehouse on Seventh Street. We only found her because it was on fire."

He replaced the pen in his jacket pocket. "Sometimes I wonder about people. Take care, Officer O'Malley."

"You too," she answered thoughtfully.

Annie found her favorite nurse, who also happened to be her sister-in-law, and begged her for a loan on a pair of hospital scrubs and a quick shower.

"Maybe the mother or father torched the warehouse so the baby would be found," her sister-in-law speculated.

"Maybe they could have left her at the bus station and she would have been found without the risk of her dying," Annie retorted.

"Still." Eileen shrugged while Annie dressed. "They might have meant well."

"In a strange sort of way," Annie agreed. "I know you see kids come through here that you wish their parents would have just dropped them off somewhere. I see them too. But this was . . ." She paused then continued. "Cold. You know what I mean? Taking a baby to an abandoned warehouse in the middle of a bunch of other abandoned buildings. What were the chances she'd be found?''

Glad to be clean, Annie took the pair of shoes Eileen offered her, even though they were wrapped in hospital sterile material. She dried her hair with a towel, wishing she had a blow-dryer with her.

''Go home and get some sleep,'' Eileen prescribed.

Annie nodded and sprayed some of the throat spray, grimacing at the taste.

''Maybe you shouldn't do that,'' Eileen teased. ''You know men like women with those throaty voices.''

Annie laughed. ''I don't think that includes sounding like a frog.''

''You don't sound like a frog,'' Eileen assured her. ''You sound very Garbo.'' She lowered her own voice dramatically.

''I'm going home,'' Annie said with a shake of her damp hair. ''This is too much for me. See you, Eileen. Thanks for the clothes and the shower.''

''Bye, Sis. See you Sunday.''

Tony Rousso was waiting at the emergency room desk when she walked out of the electronic doors. She saw him a minute before he caught her out of the corner of his eye. She started to duck back inside.

Then she remembered that she had wanted to thank him and held her bag a little tighter as she walked up to him.

Chapter Two

He was leaning negligently against the waiting room wall. Tall, dark skinned, and black haired, he wore his hair a little too long for department regulations. But it looked good on him.

He had narrow hips and a muscular chest and shoulders. It was easy to imagine him carrying people out of burning buildings. Including herself. He was in his black uniform, minus the heavy protective gear and helmet. It made him seem more approachable.

"O'Malley," he acknowledged, eyeing her carefully from her hospital shoes to the top of her damp red hair.

If his eyes lingered a little longer than they should

have around certain parts of her anatomy, she refused to take offense. The man had saved her life, after all.

"Rousso," she returned. "I'm glad I got to see you again this soon."

Dark fires lit up in the back of his black eyes and his smile was wickedly curved. "Something I can do for you, O'Malley?"

She shrugged and clutched the plastic bag that held her uniform a little tighter. "Just wanted to say thanks for saving my life."

"That's my job," he told her with a curious look. "I came to see how you and the baby were doing."

"I'm fine, just a scratchy throat. The baby seems to be okay too. They're keeping her overnight for observation, then she'll be released to social services in the morning."

"I'm glad to hear it—about both of you." He nodded, his eyes intent on her face. "You saved her life."

"That's my job," she mimicked in reply.

He looked at her again, thinking how different she looked out of uniform with her hair all damp and curling around her head. Her eyes were wide and very blue in contrast to the pale fragile lines of her face. He had never noticed that certain air of vulnerability about her before that night. It was very attractive.

"Not exactly," he argued. "But we won't get into the regulations tonight. Need a ride?" he asked carefully, ready for the quick shake of her head and the firmly spoken ''no, thanks.''

She smiled guardedly. ''No, that's okay. I already called a taxi.''

''Okay.'' He accepted her response. ''I'll see you around then, O'Malley.''

''Yeah,'' she nodded quickly. ''Thanks again, Rousso.''

Annie waited at the entrance to the hospital for the taxi she'd called. It was bitterly cold since the evening had given way to night. The wind whipped debris and dead leaves through the parking lot. She didn't dare step back inside, though. Taxi drivers were notorious for leaving any fare that wasn't exactly on the spot.

She would have slipped on her heavy jacket, but it had been so full of black soot that she rebelled at the idea. She was freezing but she was tough.

Think warm, she told herself. Think hot coffee and chestnuts roasting on open fires.

It didn't help that Rousso was sitting in his car just a few hundred yards away. He'd been there since she'd come out of the hospital some twenty minutes before. The sleek black sports car (she wasn't sure how he could afford one on a fireman's salary) sat parked with its engine running, headlights on dim.

What was he waiting for anyway? she wondered, annoyed. Why didn't he go home or something?

It would be warm in that car, she thought enviously. She could be home in twenty minutes. A ride home didn't make a commitment. She was being too prickly, too worried about what had happened between them. It had been a long time before. He was probably married and had children.

She waited another ten minutes until she was worried that her toes were going to have frostbite. She thought about her first year on the force when she'd had a date with another officer.

Stories were bandied around the squad room for months after their brief but ill-fated flirtation. It would be the same thing if someone saw her with Tony Rousso.

Not that she intended to flirt with him, she amended as she watched him drive up close to her.

She was going to take him up on his offer of a ride home, thank him politely when they got there, then put it out of her mind. Really. She couldn't even believe that she still remembered that he had asked her out three years before. Maybe she was mistaken. Maybe it wasn't Rousso, but another firefighter.

He pushed open the car door and she stepped off the curb, looking at his face in the interior light.

There was no mistaking that smile. It had been Rousso who had asked her out. She hadn't forgotten and she hadn't been mistaken.

There was something a little predatory about that smile. Something that had lingered with her for three years through her failed engagement and the unhappiness that had followed. Something that had disturbed her.

It had disturbed her when he'd asked her out to dinner. She had been dating Sean for a year. It was a serious relationship. Yet she'd felt Rousso's words tug at her. It was like she'd wanted to go with him.

"Come on, O'Malley," he urged her in the present. "It's not getting any warmer. You know taxi drivers don't like to come down here in the middle of the night."

She wanted to tell him to go on without her. She wanted to walk away. But her feet were too numb and her teeth were chattering with cold.

She climbed in beside him in the low-slung car and closed the door behind her. "Thanks."

"No problem." He started out of the parking lot.

"What made you wait?"

He looked back at her in the dim dash light. "I didn't like the idea of leaving you here. Why didn't you let your partner come for you?"

She shrugged. "He has a family. His wife gets worried."

He grinned as he pulled out into the sparse traffic. "She's worried about the two of you, isn't she?"

"I didn't say that," she retorted sharply. Even though it was true. Since the birth of their son the year before, Tom's wife had been very hostile about their partnership.

"A guy like him with a woman like you. All day. Sometimes late into the night—"

"She doesn't have anything to worry about," Annie assured him brittlely. "Tom and I are friends. That's it. I wouldn't fool around with my partner. It could be too dangerous."

"Do you mean dangerous as in exciting," he continued, "or dangerous as in hazardous?"

"Hazardous!" she exclaimed. "What is it with you?"

"It's got nothing to do with me," he told her innocently as they approached the main road. "Where to?"

"Oak Park, First and Sumner," she responded uneasily. "I can't believe you listened in on my conversation with Tom! I'm surprised you didn't ask someone where I lived before you came to the hospital."

"I knew that a taxi wouldn't come out here at this time of night," he explained, not looking at her as he turned out into heavier traffic. "Your partner did too. He might have come for you anyway and I would have wasted my time."

"Instead you decided that he was afraid because his wife thinks we might be fooling around," she surmised briefly.

"Not until he didn't show up," he agreed. "Then I knew there had to be something seriously wrong."

"And that was your first thought?"

"My only thought," he replied evenly. "Tell me I'm wrong, O'Malley, and I'll apologize for misunderstanding the situation."

Annie fought with herself. It was a valiant struggle between the truth and putting him in his place.

"Okay." She retreated with a heavy sigh. "Alice does have a problem with us being partners. But it's just because she's insecure right now. It'll be better later.''

He glanced at her. ''I can't believe you admitted it! You are one honest cop.''

''And you are one obnoxious fireman! No wonder I didn't want to consider dating you three years ago!''

''I thought you were involved?'' he asked quietly.

''I was,'' she returned bluntly. ''I'm not anymore. We had some problems and we decided we'd be better off apart.''

''What kind of problems?'' He wanted to know.

''None of your business!'' she answered, clutching her bag to her side tightly. Was he always so provoking?

''Okay,'' he relented. ''I'm sorry about your relationship, O'Malley.''

She sighed and looked out of the window at the passing city skyline. ''Me too. My parents have been married thirty-two years. I have a sister who's been married ten years. I couldn't even manage a walk down the aisle.''

He heard the pain in her voice and knew he was treading on highly volatile ground but he pressed on anyway. ''So, what's happening now? Did you find someone else?''

''No,'' she admitted. ''There might be the same problem if . . .''

''If?'' he prodded.

''If I decided to date someone seriously again,'' she ground out between her teeth. She wasn't ready to talk to him about the reason she and Sean had broken up.

They were silent for a few moments while the car waited through three lights to get to an intersection.

"Any chance you can put on that uniform and get us through this tonight?" he asked, turning his head to look at her. In the dash light, she looked like a scared twelve-year-old.

"No!" She grimaced, glad for the subject change. "I'm not even sure if this uniform can be cleaned! Now I know why you guys wear all that gear! It's the only way you can stay clean."

"That warehouse had a tar roof and old wiring," he explained. "Not that any fire isn't dirty."

She looked at him and opened her mouth to speak, then found him looking at her and turned her head quickly to glance out of her window at the dark street.

Clearly, she was uncomfortable with him, he decided, traffic moving forward again. It had been three years but not enough time to forget that stinging rebuke she had dealt him when he'd asked her out for dinner the first time he'd seen her. It was interesting that she remembered too.

"I noticed that your partner didn't follow you into the warehouse when he thought you might be down."

She dared another glance at him. He was looking at the road and she took an instant to trace his profile with her eyes. He was a very attractive man. Like

Sean, he was probably very aware of that fact and used it to his advantage.

"I guess that was a good thing or you would have had to carry both of us out," she said casually. "Tom's a good man. But he's a stickler for the rules."

"And you're not?" he guessed with a trace of a smile in his voice. "Annie O'Malley, Irish rebel?"

"Not exactly," she disagreed. "But my parents would agree with that. I was the only girl in my family to take the shield even though all my brothers and my father are all on the force. Two of my sisters are full-time parents and the third is a dental hygienist. They're the good girls, I suppose."

"I think what you did tonight was pretty good stuff," he said in a deep voice that raced along her spine. "Even though it was a little out of the rule book."

"What about you?" she asked, turning the tables on him. "Do you always follow the rules?"

"Always," he replied calmly. "Unless I need to break them."

She laughed and he thought she might be starting to relax. She wasn't clutching that bag as though her life depended on it anymore. That had to be a good sign.

"Which building?" he asked when he'd turned down her street.

"The one on the right," she answered, surprised that the ride had passed so quickly. She hadn't expected to actually enjoy talking with him. It was even more of a surprise to feel her pulses racing and to find herself sneaking looks at him. She felt like a kid again.

He pulled the car into a parking space near her door. The headlight beams shone brightly through the cold night air.

"Thanks for the ride home," she said as she swung her legs out of the car.

That's it, she reminded herself. You don't have to go any further.

"No problem," he answered quickly.

Maybe he just wasn't her type, he speculated. It was good he found out quickly. It wasn't that he'd carried a torch for her for three years. Seeing her again had reminded him that he'd never had the chance to get to know her. Maybe it was just as well.

Annie glanced at him. She couldn't have said afterward what made her do it but she said, "I'm going to make some coffee."

"Are you asking me in?" he responded, staring at her.

"Unless you have something better to do," she allowed, fumbling for her keys while the wind whipped around her thin hospital gear.

The car engine died and she heard the door open and close just as she dropped her bag and had to lunge for one of her shoes as it rolled under the side of the car.

He picked up the keys when she dropped them on the curb and unlocked the door to her apartment, standing aside to allow her into the dark room before him.

"Only my report on the fire today," he answered as she brushed past him and snapped on a lamp near the door.

"There's no way you can write it without saying that I bent the regs," she concluded, tingling from the brief touch of his chest against her side.

He handed her the keys to her apartment. "As far as I'm concerned, you and I went in together. You were overpowered. I took you both out."

"Why?" she demanded, watching him close the front door. "Why would you do that for me?" She studied him closely when she'd switched on a light. "If you think that I'll be grateful enough to—"

He held up a large, well-shaped hand. "I think you did what you had to do tonight. I don't see any reason for you to be called for it. Nothing more. Okay?"

"Sorry," she admitted sheepishly, not realizing exactly how small her apartment was until they were both standing in the living area. "I just thought—"

"I know what you thought," he said bluntly. "I asked you out once, O'Malley. I haven't spent the last three years following you around and stealing your lingerie! I'm not going to pounce on you now."

She nodded, feeling acutely stupid. "I'm not myself with the fire and everything." She made inane excuses for her attitude.

"Smoke inhalation will do that to you," he pardoned easily. "Nice place," he remarked, changing the awkward subject, looking around her tiny home.

"If you don't mind living in a dollhouse," she answered brightly. "Where do you live?"

"About a block from the station house. I was lucky enough to get in on one of those reclaiming deals, so I bought a house. Low interest, free remodeling."

"One of those older neighborhoods they're always trying to get us to move into and kick out the drug dealers?"

"Something like that," he agreed. "The drug dealers have been gone for years now. It's pretty quiet."

"It must be nice to have so much room," she commented self-consciously. Her apartment was a kitchen and a living room with a sofa that turned into a bed and a closet that had been converted into a bathroom.

"It is," he said, looking around her apartment with interest. There was a lot someone could tell about a person by the way they lived and the things they owned.

"I'll start the coffee," she promised, walking through the living room. "Have a seat."

The apartment was clean but sparsely furnished. It looked as though she didn't really live there. A small television was in one corner and a bookshelf was in the other. There was a large Mexican sombrero hanging from the ceiling and a half-dead plant on the windowsill.

Annie turned on the kitchen light, watching him look at her things. Wondering what he saw when he was looking at them. She was glad that she hadn't eaten at home the night before so there were no dishes in the sink. She'd taken the time to put her bed back in place that morning before she'd left for work.

"Something I can do to help?" he offered, following her into the kitchen.

She rinsed out the spare cup that she saved for guests. "Do you take milk in your coffee?"

"No, I like it straight," he returned with a shrug. "Something from my Italian upbringing. My mother makes espresso hot and black. I'm used to drinking coffee that way."

"Just as well," she returned when she'd opened the refrigerator door. "I'm out of milk."

"How about you?" he asked, standing very close to her in the kitchen that was little more than a cubbyhole.

"Me?" she wondered, baffled as she looked at him. His eyes were very dark with thick, curling black lashes that fringed them.

"Milk in your coffee," he reminded her, enjoying her momentary look of bewilderment.

"Oh no," she answered, smiling, feeling foolish that she had been staring at him. "I mean, I don't care if there's milk or not."

The water perked through the beans and the filter and the hot, brown liquid pushed into the glass pot below it. The noise distracted Annie and she rushed forward to grab the cups. One of them, her good one, dropped from the cabinet like a stone and would have smashed on the tile floor.

But he caught it and held it out to her with a smile on his handsome features.

"Nice catch," she commented wryly, her fingers colliding with his as she took the cup from him.

He looked up into her face with a curious expression. "Glad that I could be there."

She poured the coffee with an unsteady hand, then watched him as he stirred in three teaspoons of sugar.

"I like it sweet," he remarked, feeling her eyes on him.

She put one teaspoon into hers, then led the way back into the living room. She sat down in the rocking chair and let him have the love seat.

"You have a commendation," he noticed as he looked up to see the plaque on the wall. "Rush into another fire?"

"No," she replied after a sip of her coffee. "Threw myself in front of a bullet."

He stared at her. "And you've managed to stay alive as a rookie for five years?"

She shrugged. "I was lucky. The shooter wasn't such a good aim."

"No wonder your partner lives by the rules."

She nodded. "I know. Poor Tom. He's terrified when he's with me."

He looked at her and they both laughed. "He's probably just afraid he won't be as lucky as you."

"Probably," she agreed, her smile lingering.

"He's lucky to have you though," Tony said, intrigued by that hint of a smile on her lips. "You'd go to bat for him. Like you did for that little girl tonight.''

She sipped her coffee, feeling a rush of heat to her face at his deeply spoken, intent words. ''I do what needs to be done.''

He shook his head. ''You went one step more, O'Malley.''

She felt herself getting lost in his eyes, that shiny blackness drawing her close. ''I . . . uh . . . is the coffee all right?''

''Great,'' he said, watching her draw away, knowing he would like to feel those smiling lips under his.

''Uh, well.'' She sipped her coffee and tried to work around it. ''You know all about my family. What do your parents do?''

He shrugged. ''My mother cooks for everyone and makes sure she puts her two cents into everyone else's business. My dad is a fire chief on the East Side. I only have one sister and she stays home with her three kids. Her husband is a smoke eater too. So are my three older brothers.''

''Your family is as out of balance as mine,'' she commented.

''Out of balance?'' he questioned, remembering suddenly that he held a cup of coffee and taking a sip from it.

''No accountants or doctors,'' she replied. ''Just like my family. When we have dinner together, we sit around talking about the force and the cases we've handled that week. It must be the same at your house.''

"Except for talking about the kids, that's true," he agreed.

"How long have you been a firefighter?" she asked after a few moments of silence between them.

"About seven years now."

"No injuries? No burning buildings falling on you?"

"Only once," he said with a frown. "I learned to get out of the way. Fast."

"Sounds like you must be lucky too," she considered.

He glanced down into the hot coffee. "In some ways."

The phone rang and she scrambled to answer it, spilling her coffee as she went, knocking the phone off the hook. They both bent down at the same time to try to clean up the mess, bumping into each other, then sitting back.

"Hello?" she managed, aware that her voice sounded a little breathy. She wouldn't want to work with this man, she decided, annoyed with her response to his close proximity. Her days would be numbered if this was the best she could do when he was around.

It was just the memory of him asking her out and the way she'd refused, she told herself. Once it was cleared up between them, there wouldn't be that odd catch in her throat or that terrible nervousness.

"Hi, Mom." She carried the phone into the kitchen. "Can I call you back in a few minutes?"

"What's the matter with your voice, Annie? Is your throat burned? I can hardly hear you!"

"I'm fine," she assured her mother. "I'll call you back and explain. Okay?"

Her mother hung up and Annie returned to the living room to find him standing up, empty coffee cup in hand, ready to leave.

"Thanks for the coffee," he said. "I should probably go and let you get some rest. Smoke inhalation can take its toll."

"It's mostly my throat," she said, clearing the raspy sound again. "I'm sure I'll be fine."

"I hope they find the little girl's parents," he said softly, looking down into her eyes and wishing he had more time to spend with her.

"I hope so," she agreed. Her hand flew to her mouth. "I forgot! There was a note taped to the carrier."

She bent down and rummaged through the plastic bag, coming back up with filthy hands and a darkened piece of paper.

"What does it say?" he wondered as she spread it out, trying not to rip it.

"I think it says 'Sara Smile,' " she replied.

He looked across her shoulder. "I think you're right. Isn't that an old song title?"

She felt his warm breath stir the tendrils of hair at the side of her neck and shivered, taking a step away from him. "I . . . uh . . . yes, I think so. Maybe her name is Sara as well. It's something to go on anyway."

"Maybe," he acceded. "Well, thanks for the coffee, O'Malley. Are you working tomorrow?"

"Tomorrow afternoon. Thanks for the ride home, Rousso."

He put his hand on the doorknob and started to open the portal.

"Tony?"

He looked back at her, surprised that she had called him by his given name. It was the first time she'd acknowledged that he had one. "Yes?"

"About that . . . uh . . . thing three years ago," she began, feeling everything twist around inside of her. She wanted to end the bad feeling between them but she didn't want him to think she was coming on to him. She didn't want to date him, just know that she didn't have to avoid him either.

"You mean when I asked you out and you bit my head off?" he finished for her with a crooked smile.

Her face flushed. "That's the thing. I was going through some disgusting stuff with my fiancé. I didn't mean to . . ." She scuffed her foot on the threadbare carpet and looked down, not able to sustain eye contact with him. ". . . bite your head off. I just wanted things to be right between us."

He reached out and touched her chin with his finger, bringing her gaze back up to meet his. "That's okay. Everything's right between us, Annie. Don't worry."

"Thanks," she whispered, feeling drawn to him again, leaning ever so slightly toward him as she stared into his eyes.

"You're welcome," he finished and moved his hand away from her face. "I'll see you around."

"You too," she added, biting her lip and pushing a strand of hair back behind one ear. "Don't work too hard."

He smiled and left her there at the door. She watched as he climbed back into his car and sped off into the night. She closed the door, wondering if she looked like some idiot hanging out the door watching him leave.

She locked the door and turned off the lights, pulling out the sofa bed and getting ready to call it a night.

She felt better, she told herself, pulling up the blanket and snuggling down into the sheets. She'd cleared up that feeling between her and Tony Rousso. There wouldn't be any more misunderstandings about it. She could forget about it and get on with her life.

So why was her heart still pounding and why did she still feel the imprint of his fingers on her chin?

Chapter Three

"What will happen now?" Annie asked the less than forthcoming woman at the social service office.

"The baby Jane Doe will be kept at the hospital until suitable accommodations can be found for her."

Annie had stopped by to check on any progress they might have made on finding Sara a place to stay.

It had been two days since they'd brought her in from the warehouse fire. There were no leads on her parents and no other relatives had appeared, even though Sara's story had made front-page news.

Annie had made copies of the note she'd found attached to the carrier. She'd distributed them at the precinct as well as with the social service people. Nothing seemed to help.

"She needs a home," Annie said with determination. "She can't live at the hospital forever."

The woman looked up at her from her desk. Her brown eyes were annoyed. "I'm well aware of that, Officer O'Malley. Believe me, we're trying to find someone we can trust with her. But right now, we're filled over capacity. This week alone we've sent seven children to out-of-state facilities. That's how bad it is."

"Can't someone just double up?"

"You don't understand the system or how it works, Officer," the woman charged. "You can't just double up on children. They each have to have their own bedroom and bathroom."

"I never had my own bedroom until I left home!" Annie argued, astonished that sharing a bedroom would take precedence over a child staying at the hospital.

"Officer—"

"What about if I find someone to take care of her? Someone with an extra bedroom?" she questioned, thinking of her parents.

"Are they certified as foster parents?"

"No," Annie answered truthfully. "But how difficult can that be?"

"There's the paperwork and the inspection and the verification of the people in question. Are they trustworthy? Can they handle taking care of a child?"

Annie stared at the woman, who stared back at her. "There is a baby in the county hospital. They don't have room for her on the nursery floor, so they have her in the ward with older people. People with contagious diseases. People who are dying. How can you be so rigid?''

The woman pursed her lips, studying the always growing pile of paperwork on her desk. She looked back at her nemesis. ''Officer O'Malley, I didn't put her there and I'd like nothing better than to get her out of the hospital and you out of my office. But without the proper situation, it's impossible.''

Annie glared at her one last time. ''Thanks for your help, Mrs. Jenkins. I'm sure Sara will be much better now.''

She stalked out of the stark, green-walled social service office, and sank down on a bench outside the door. The sun was warm that afternoon even though the wind was cold, tugging at her clean jacket and cap.

She had talked to everyone she could think of to talk to about Sara. No one seemed interested enough to help her. They were all too worried about their rules and regulations.

To her mind, any home would be better than the ward she'd visited Sara in that morning. She was a baby. She shouldn't have been around sick and dying people.

Sara had smiled at her that morning and made soft cooing noises when she'd grasped Annie's finger in her little fist. The nurse had said she was about three pounds underweight but otherwise unharmed. She was taking formula well and, if there was time, they could find some cereal for her. That would help her put on some weight.

The nurse also showed Annie Sara's first baby tooth. Annie had exclaimed over it and held the little girl tightly. She had to find some way to get her out of that hospital.

"Annie!" Someone hailed her from the street.

She watched Tony sprint lightly up the stairs. He was wearing blue jeans and a gray jacket. She had never noticed the smile lines beside his eyes before. Or the way her pulse bumped when she saw him.

"Tony," she answered. "What brings you over here?"

He shrugged. "I've been keeping up with Sara. I've been to the hospital every day, hoping she wouldn't be there. I can't believe they haven't found her a home. So, I came over here to see—"

"Mrs. Jenkins?" she guessed, shielding her eyes from the sun to look up at him. "That's where I spent the last twenty minutes."

He frowned as she explained what the social worker had told her. "There has to be a better answer," he agreed.

"I know," Annie fumed. "I just don't know what it is."

He glanced down at his gloved hands. "I might know. I'm going in there to offer to foster Sara myself."

Annie's eyes grew wide in her wind-reddened face. "How will you take care of her?"

"I've helped out with kids at home and I've been an uncle for several years. I think I could manage."

"Great," she enthused while she berated herself for not thinking of it. "I'd like to go in with you, if you don't mind."

"That's fine," he answered. "I just want to get this over with and get Sara out of there."

Annie took a seat in the waiting room while Tony told the secretary who he was and that he wanted to see Mrs. Jenkins.

She was amazed and pleased to find that he had been as worried as she had been about Sara. Surely, between the two of them, they could keep her from getting lost in the system.

Mrs. Jenkins opened the door to her office and greeted him. "You called about fostering the baby Jane Doe in the hospital," she acknowledged, taking his hand. "You were part of the team that brought her in from the warehouse, I understand."

"That's right," he replied confidently. He glanced at Annie, who smiled encouragingly.

Mrs. Jenkins saw her and sighed. "You might as well come in too, Officer O'Malley. Are the two of you in on this together?"

They exchanged confiding looks. "Not exactly," Annie replied.

"No," Tony told her. "We're both just interested."

Annie accompanied Tony back into the green office and they took seats in front of Mrs. Jenkins's desk.

"I don't want to make this any harder than it has to be," the woman told them, "contrary to what Officer O'Malley thinks."

Tony frowned at Annie as she was about to speak. "I'm sure Officer O'Malley is just worried about Sara."

Mrs. Jenkins smiled in an unpleasant way. "I'm sure she is. Now, Mr. Rousso, are you qualified to be a foster parent?"

He shrugged. "I'm not sure. I have plenty of experience with children. I have a large house with plenty of room. I make a good salary. Is there anything else?"

Mrs. Jenkins eyed him prospectively. "Well, since you are a member of the fire department and, I'm assuming, an upstanding member of the community, the process could be shortened. What about your wife?"

"My wife?" he asked.

"Yes," Mrs. Jenkins continued, "how does she feel about fostering the baby? What does she do for a living?"

Tony exchanged glances with Annie. "I'm not married."

Mrs. Jenkins stared at him. "You're not . . . and you thought you could foster the baby?"

He nodded. "A good friend of mine just adopted a little boy. He's single. Is there a difference?"

"I afraid so, Mr. Rousso. You have to be a married couple to foster a child."

"Or she has to stay in the hospital?" he demanded.

Mrs. Jenkins drew in a deep breath. "As I just explained to Officer O'Malley." She turned her gaze to Annie. "You aren't married, are you, Officer?"

"No," Annie replied quietly.

"Then I'm afraid there's no help for the child from either of you. I'll be willing to talk to any couple you find suitable, particularly if they are police or fire department personnel. We could probably dispense with a lot of the paperwork if they were qualified."

Annie got out of her chair quickly and walked out of the door without another word.

"Thanks, Mrs. Jenkins," Tony said, shaking the other woman's hand. "I know you're only doing your job."

"I wish you'd tell her!" She nodded toward the door that Annie had just walked through.

Tony found her outside again, staring into the dying sunlight as the sun dropped behind the city skyline.

"Sorry." He sank down beside her on the step. "I thought I had the answer."

She shrugged. "I'll have to talk to some of my married friends. See if they could spare some room."

"I could do that too," he agreed. "There has to be a way."

She nodded. "Well, we tried. Sometimes the system doesn't work."

"Most of the time, it's for the best," he replied. "If they did just let anyone have the children, they'd be no better off than they were with their abusive parents. They're trying to make it better for them.''

Annie yawned and stood up. ''I'm off-duty until Monday morning,'' she announced. ''I think I'm going to grab some dinner and go back to sleep until then.''

''That's a long time to sleep,'' he teased, standing beside her. ''Maybe I'm just jealous. I'm only off until tomorrow.''

She laughed. ''I just got off of a double shift so I don't feel sorry for you. Everybody has this flu thing so the rest of us have to suffer for being well.''

''I know what you mean,'' he replied. ''Half of the station didn't show up for roll call today.''

''Maybe we should both call in sick just to get even,'' she suggested, starting down the concrete steps toward her squad car.

''Annie?'' he called as she removed her hat and her copper tresses spilled out across her shoulders.

She looked up at him and smiled, waiting for him to speak.

''Have dinner with me.''

Despite the fact that she had hoped it had been laid to rest between them, there were still traces of that moment three years ago when they'd first met at a fire where she was doing crowd control and he was working the hose.

It hadn't been any more involved than that, she supposed. Hi, I'm Tony Rousso. Have dinner with me.

She'd felt his gaze on her and felt jarred by his words, wanting to go with him, despite herself.

Three years ago, she'd blasted him for trying to take advantage of the situation, for being a man at a time when she was beginning to think that all men were liars and heartless flirts.

She studied him closely. "That took some awesome courage."

"Not really." He smiled back at her, then walked down the steps to where she stood with her car door open, the wind blowing her hair across her shoulder. "You don't scare me, Annie."

"I'm wearing a gun," she offered, her mouth feeling dry and her stomach fluttering.

"I'll pick you up in two hours," he retorted, his eyes steady on hers. "Wear your gun, if it makes you feel safer."

He waited patiently, one hand on the car door, the wind whipping at his dark hair.

"Don't be late," she replied finally, sliding into the car seat.

He shut the door tightly, smiled at her through the glass, then walked back to his own car.

Annie's sister had borrowed her only good dress. She rummaged through the rest of her clothes, discarding everything she came into contact with until she had only a quarter of an hour left before Tony would be there.

Finally, she had no choice but to put on a well-worn green wool dress. She bit her lip when she saw that it made her skin look pasty white in contrast. She put on some makeup, pinched her cheeks, and brushed her hair.

It wasn't a date after all, she told herself. It was more two co-workers getting together for dinner. They were sure to spend the evening talking about Sara and telling each other harrowing stories about their jobs.

She looked at her hair, trying to decide if she should wear it up or down. She frowned. It wasn't a date. If she wore it down, it would probably just get in the way. Better to pin it back.

The doorbell rang and she looked at her watch. It was him! Maybe it wasn't a date but her stomach was in knots and she couldn't maneuver her hands to fasten the clip in her hair.

"I'm just getting my coat," she said when she let him in the door.

"No gun?" he queried, his eyes approving her long legs in the short dress and the sweeping length of her hair loose on her shoulders.

She put on her coat and brushed by him. "I'm not afraid of you either, Tony," she repeated his own words. "Let's eat."

For an instant, he was stunned by her flashing eyes and beautiful lips. Then he closed the door behind him and followed her to the car.

She'd expected Italian for dinner. He took her to a new salsa club where the music was loud and the food was spicy. They ordered dinner and he stood up, taking her hand and walking her out to the dance floor.

The pulsating rhythms were wild and hot. Annie didn't know if she could move fast enough as she looked at the other dancers.

"Follow me," Tony said in her ear, putting one hand on her waist and taking hold of her hand with the other.

They moved well together. It took her only a moment to catch on to the breathless tempo. She laughed as he spun her until she was dizzy but she didn't miss a step.

It was easy, really. Even though she was never much of a dancer. He caught her in his arms and laid her back away from him, his eyes laughing and watching her. `

"Don't drop me!" she squealed, uncertain about the close proximity of the floor.

"I'm a fireman," he reminded her in mock offense. "I never drop anyone."

The music slowed and the lights dimmed. She went easily into his arms, pressing closely against him without thinking.

He smelled of soap and aftershave and she turned her face into the hollow of his neck while he held her as though she were some fragile flower that might be damaged.

Annie felt light, vulnerable, excited, when she moved with him across the floor. She put her arms around his neck and let him move them, slowly, one of his hands resting lightly on her hip.

The dance seemed to last for a long time as they shared the floor with several other couples. Annie closed her eyes and felt his touch on her back, his breath in her hair. They were barely moving enough to call it dancing but she didn't care.

It was wonderful being held without having to think about the consequences. It was good to feel his warmth against her. She didn't know him that well but she trusted him. He had saved her life. But there was something more. Something less defined, yet just as powerful.

She lifted her head. The lights were barely shadows. His eyes were intent on hers and his face was very near her own.

"Annie," he whispered, his lips close to her mouth as he spoke her name.

She felt an excited tremor run through her, moving her a little closer to him. She wanted to feel his mouth against hers.

The lights came up and the band made a trilling sound, shouting out loud as the music changed and the frantic beat resumed itself on the dance floor. Couples crowded around them and the lights flashed in time to the music.

Annie blinked her eyes, disoriented, and smiled self-consciously, glancing at their table. "I think we should eat," she said to him over the din. "I don't think I can dance anymore without food."

He kept her hand trapped in his and led her toward their table, through the people writhing and stomping on the wooden floor.

There was a ton of food on their plates and Annie

didn't know where to start with it all. Part of her was still very aware of her partner across the table.

"This is so much," she said, picking up her fork. "It looks like enough for a whole family."

"If it is," he remarked, picking up his fork, "they must be living in my stomach!"

They both managed to make a considerable dent in the food and sat back, replete. They had spent the time talking about Sara, as Annie had predicted, but they hadn't come up with an answer.

"She's already been through so much," Annie said, shaking her head. "It's not fair."

"I agree," he replied. "I just don't know how to help her."

In mutual consent, they drove to the hospital, leaving the dance club and the loud music behind. The afternoon shift was just changing, the nurses trying to catch up with everything. They were glad when Tony and Annie offered to feed the baby, who was crying as they came into the ward.

"I don't know what we're doing with her down here anyway," one nurse grumbled loudly.

Annie put on a hospital gown over her dress and picked up the crying baby. Sara stopped at once and looked up at her with hopeful eyes.

The nurse sighed and put the bottle of formula into Annie's hand. "I'll be on my rounds. Call me before you leave."

Tony found a big, comfortable chair and Annie snuggled the baby into her arm, putting the bottle to her hungry mouth.

"She is beautiful," Annie said, touching Sara's hands and face. "How could anyone desert her?"

Tony sat perched on the wide arm of the chair beside her, his hip brushing her arm as he watched her feed the baby.

"It happens," he murmured softly, reaching down to caress the baby's downy head. "People get into trouble. Relationships don't work out. The children are always hurt."

She glanced up at him. "You sound like a social worker," she remarked, surprised at the depth and tone of understanding in his voice. "People like us, with big families and parents who love us, sometimes forget that there are babies that no one wants."

He frowned and she watched his eyes grow darker.

"Some people like us are those children," he told her. "My father rescued me and my mother from a closet in a third-story rat trap in Cicero when I was five years old. She died before they could get her to the hospital."

"What are you saying?" Annie asked him, staring at the dark line of his face.

He looked at her and smiled grimly. "I remember my parents arguing. I remember my father leaving my mother and telling me that I could have her if I could put up with her. When she died, Angelo Rousso adopted me, gave me his name, and made me a member of his family. But I've never forgotten."

"Tony," Annie sympathized, putting her hand on his as she imagined him as a dark-haired little boy. "I'm sorry. I didn't know."

"Not a lot of people do," he said. "The Roussos are my family. They've never treated me any different than the other kids. But I remember my birth parents' anger and their bitterness with one another." He looked down at Sara and the darkness left his face. "I'm glad she won't be able to remember."

Annie kept her eyes on Sara as she finished her bottle, understanding why Tony had a special feeling for the baby.

"You were one of the lucky ones, though," she reminded him. "So many children aren't ever wanted."

He nodded and stared down at Sara. "It'll be awhile before anyone could adopt Sara, even if her mother or father don't come back."

"I know." She looked back down at the baby. "I wish it would have worked out that one of us could have been her foster parent until then."

Tony's eyes narrowed on her face. "There's lots of eligible people out there. We just have to find the right ones. We could work on it together in our off hours."

Annie put the sleeping baby in her crib. It made sense, the two of them working together to find little Sara a home. The only thing that bothered her was the awareness she had of him. That feeling when she was around him that made it hard to breathe or speak. She didn't want to have a relationship with Tony Rousso but maybe they could help Sara.

"We could do that," she agreed finally.

"Tough decision?" he wondered at the time lapse.

"Sara's asleep," she whispered. "We can talk about it in the car."

They left Sara sleeping in the battered hospital crib and Tony took her home, each of them lost in their own thoughts about the task that they had committed to that evening.

"It's late," he said at her door. "I have to be at the station early."

Annie nodded. "It's not that I don't want to help Sara," she explained bluntly. "And I do think we could be more effective working together. It's just that . . ."

"What?" he asked, mystified by her silence and her lack of enthusiasm.

"I don't want to get involved with you," she said carefully. "I just got out of a bad relationship. I don't want another one right away."

Tony looked at her face in the streetlight's glare. "What makes you think it would be another bad one?"

She shrugged. "I don't want to find out."

"I see," he admitted. "You feel like there's some danger of that? Us getting involved?"

"I don't know," she replied. "I just wanted to be up front with you about it."

"I appreciate the thought. And I'll try to keep focused on the job."

"I'll call you Monday," she insisted, "and we can set the whole thing up."

He wrote down his phone number on the back of a matchbook.

"Sounds good. I'm off Monday, Thursday, and Saturday next week but I work twelves the rest of the week."

"Am I supposed to be the one doing all the changing for this partnership?" she demanded.

He laughed. "You fit your schedule in next week, I'll fit mine the week after and so on until we find Sara a home. Okay?"

"That works," she agreed, holding out her hand.

"I guess we'll take it as it comes, Annie." He shook her hand lightly and held it. "Do you want to kiss me?"

"What?" she demanded, that breathless feeling coming over her quickly.

"A friendly kiss," he explained quickly. "Nothing personal or anything."

His hand was warm on hers and she felt her face heating up as well. "Maybe that's not such a good idea, Tony."

"We can't kiss without getting involved?" he asked. "Is there something else you want to tell me, O'Malley? Like how you've had this crush on me for a long time and your blood pressure goes up at the sight of me and—"

"I can kiss you," she answered, cutting him off. "It's no big deal."

They looked at each other. Tony tugged at her hand a little and she moved closer to him.

"It's no big deal," she repeated.

"Well then, put your mouth where the money is, sweetheart," he quipped.

Her heart was pounding wildly. She felt light-headed and breathless but she pushed all of her feelings aside and put her mouth against his.

Their lips were cool from the cold night air. His warmed at once from the contact and she felt herself being drawn against him. Her whole world began to slip away and she felt her arms move up to his neck.

Quickly she broke away, opening her door and slipping inside as she mumbled something about calling him later.

The feeling of her lips on his mouth lingered, as did the scent of her perfume. Tony already had more than friendly feelings for Annie.

He looked at the closed apartment door and smiled. There was always tomorrow.

Chapter Four

"I can't believe you're dating a fireman," her mother said with a shake of her graying head. "Surely there's enough young officers on your own squad—"

"We're not dating, Mom," Annie argued.

It was Sunday. The shouts of encouragement from the den were for the football game that her father and brothers were watching.

Two of her brothers were on duty in a few hours but everyone came for dinner. Her sisters were upstairs, napping with their babies. Her sisters-in-law had left after dinner to visit their own families.

"You're not dating," her mother repeated.

"No, we're working on a project together, finding

a home for that little baby we found in the abandoned warehouse,'' Annie continued to explain.

She had waited until after dinner to talk with her mother, hoping she could stop any speculation about Tony when her brothers saw them together. It was bound to happen.

''You're working together? Long hours, outside the job, that kind of thing?''

''Yes, but—''

''You're going to get yourself in trouble with him,'' her mother predicted.

''What's up with you two?'' her father asked, coming into the kitchen for another beer.

''Your daughter is dating again,'' Katie O'Malley told her husband.

''That's good,'' he expressed his happiness with a lift of the beer after he had opened it. ''Who's the man?''

''Tony Rousso. But we're not dating,'' Annie explained again. ''We're working together.''

''Rousso, Rousso,'' her father considered. ''What squad's he in?''

''He's a fireman,'' Katie said.

''A fireman?'' Mike exclaimed. ''You're dating a fireman?''

''I'm not dating him! We're trying to find a home for the baby we rescued from the warehouse.'' Annie tried to make them understand.

Her father nodded grimly. ''The one where you broke the regs and waltzed into a burning building.''

''Who told you?'' Annie demanded.

"Walked into a burning building! I can't believe it! If you're not trying to stop a bullet with your hard head, you're trying to set yourself on fire!"

"What's up?" Her brother, Patrick, joined them in the kitchen.

"Nothing!" Annie exclaimed defensively.

"Your sister is dating a fireman," her parents told him.

Annie walked out of the kitchen.

It had seemed like such a good idea. Tell everyone what was going on and save herself a lot of trouble. Word got around fast in the department. It wouldn't take long for people to see her with Tony on the street.

Somehow, it had all gone wrong.

She sat down on the swing on her mother's front porch and watched the children playing basketball in the drive. Annie had grown up in that house, playing basketball in the yard and riding her bike in the street. Her brothers had protected her from the bullies in the neighborhood when they weren't beating her up themselves.

She had learned young that they knew everything and what she didn't tell them, they found out anyway. Her two older brothers had roughed up her first boyfriend, Tommy Allen, and he hadn't come for her birthday party.

"Telephone, Annie," Patrick yelled from the kitchen. "I think it's the fireman."

She sighed and went back inside, taking the phone

from her brother. He grinned at her, then stood with her parents, waiting to hear her conversation.

"Annie?"

"Yeah, Tony," she answered uncomfortably.

"I got a lead on a good place for Sara. My brother told me about this home where they take babies and handle adoption. I'm off in three hours. Want to take a ride out there with me?"

Three pairs of eyes were watching her. She twisted the phone cord around her finger.

Should she go out there with him? He could check out the place without her. If she went with him every time he called, there was going to be more talk.

On the other hand, hadn't they agreed that they would work together and didn't that mean looking over the place together and trying to find Sara a home?

"Annie? Yoo hoo? Are you still there?" Tony asked on the line.

Patrick smiled at her and her mother frowned.

"Yeah, I'm off the rest of the day and not on again until tomorrow afternoon. I'd like to go," she said with a defiant turn of her head away from her audience.

Her mother turned away with a shake of her head and her father frowned and walked away.

"Annie? Is everything okay?" Tony wondered.

"Fine. Everything's fine," she replied tautly. "I'll meet you."

"Can you drive? My car's got bad brakes."

"Sure. I'll pick you up," she suggested, trying to

think of somewhere out of the way that they could meet.

"Okay, I'll be at the station house. See you."

The phone went dead in her hand. She hung up the receiver. So much for keeping their relationship low profile. By tomorrow, everyone would think they were dating.

"This can only bring trouble," her mother told her from the recesses of the huge old pantry.

"It won't cause anything," Annie promised. "We're just friends. Not even friends. Just working together."

Her father nodded curtly. "Bring him for dinner."

Annie paled. "Dad, I—"

"Bring him," he ordered, shaking his head still bright with red hair like her own. "We'll see if he measures up. It'll be hard for a fireman."

Annie shook her head, deciding to go home first and change clothes before she met Tony. Patrick and John met her in the hallway.

"Fireman, huh?"

"Don't start with me," she told them.

Both brothers laughed. "Scared we'll run him off?"

"No."

"Maybe you should be. He doesn't have a gun. Maybe he could bring his fire hose."

They laughed all the way back to the den where she could hear them repeating the joke to the rest of her family.

Annie picked up her sweater and purse, then hugged her mother. "I'm going."

"Be careful," her mother warned. "That last one almost broke your heart. He wasn't on the force either."

Annie looked into her mother's eyes, so like her own. "I know, Mom. I'll be careful."

"Bring him for dinner!" her father yelled as she was walking out the door.

Annie grimaced and closed the door behind her.

Back at her apartment, she changed the dress she'd worn to church that morning. She put on a new blue sweater her mother had given her for Christmas and a pair of black wool slacks that her sister said looked good on her.

She made a face at herself in the mirror. She didn't want to know what her family would make of her thumping pulse and flushed cheeks. It didn't matter. They were only working together to find Sara a home.

She also knew that the kiss they had exchanged was just friendly. She had only kissed him to show him that it didn't matter. And it would never happen again.

It was that whole thing about him asking her out, she decided, as she drove to the station house to meet him. If that hadn't happened between them, she wouldn't have thought about him that way.

Why had he wanted to kiss her? she asked herself for the hundredth time. Why had she kissed him back?

She was going to have to do better than this if she was going to keep her relationship with him professional. What would Tony make of it if she always wore her uniform to remind herself?

He was waiting on the curb outside the station. His hair was wet as though he had recently showered and he was wearing his street clothes. He looked good to her. Too good.

The men and women inside the station paused to get a good look at them while they were loading supplies on a fire truck. Good-natured laughing and pointing followed.

Annie wished that she had worn dark glasses. A few of them had worked with her. They were going to recognize her.

"Ignore them," Tony advised, getting into the car. "All of them need to get lives of their own."

"There's something about being single," Annie agreed, pulling away from the curb and the firefighters. "Everybody has a stake in your life."

"Don't I know it," he remarked. "All I did was pick you up at the hospital and I've got my father, mother, and three uncles breathing down my neck for information about you."

Annie could understand that feeling.

"Where are we going?" she asked.

"It's about two hours outside of town," he told her, "but it sounds like a great place. My brother says it's a real working farm. The couple take in foster children and have nine adopted kids of their own."

"That sounds great," she agreed. "Are they taking in any other kids?"

"I talked with them this morning. It sounded like they could be interested in adopting Sara."

"Wow!" she replied enthusiastically. "That would be great. She would have a ready-made family. No skipping around from place to place."

"That's what I was thinking. They said they've been looking for another baby to adopt. Sara could be as good as any other baby."

It was slow going getting out of the city. Late-afternoon traffic was heavy since the weather was getting cold. It didn't help that half the lanes on the expressway were closed for construction.

"Looks like snow, huh?" Tony asked after their initial conversation had lagged for several minutes.

"Yeah," Annie agreed. "It's cold enough to snow."

"I know I'm crazy," he told her. "I like snow. I know it's messy and makes traffic worse but I like it anyway."

She glanced at him and smiled. "I do too. It reminds me of being a kid and going sledding in the park."

"Reminds you? You don't sled anymore?" he wondered, looking at her profile as she concentrated on the road.

"I haven't been sledding since I was sixteen and decided that falling off your sled didn't make you attractive to boys," she told him with a laugh. "I was too cool."

Tony smiled, imagining her as a skinny girl with freckles and carrot red hair trying to impress boys.

"Guys can be cool and still have fun," he answered. "We're lucky."

"Yeah, you don't have makeup to ruin and you can just run your hand through your hair and it looks okay."

Annie turned on to the expressway out of the city. She was so aware of Tony sitting at her side that her spine hurt from holding her back so straight.

Every time she looked at him she thought about kissing him; how his mouth had felt, how she had felt. It wasn't something she wanted to think about.

"What do you think?" Tony asked.

Annie realized that she had been so intent on not thinking about him that she had been thinking intently about him. So intently that she had totally missed what he had said to her.

"I'm sorry?" She admitted that she hadn't heard him.

"I know traffic's bad, Annie," he said with a smile, "but that scowl on your face is scaring the guy next to us."

Annie glanced at her face in the rearview mirror. She did look as though she were about to hit someone. She purposely eased the lines from between her brows and relaxed her mouth.

"I was . . . uh . . . thinking about something," she said quietly, hoping he wouldn't ask what.

"Not food, I take it?" he asked cheerfully, wondering what she had been thinking about.

"Food?"

"I was asking you how you felt about getting something to eat. I'm starving."

"Oh, sure," she replied guiltily. "We could do that."

"Wherever you want to stop is fine," he told her.

She stopped at a small restaurant just off the expressway that she knew had good food and pretty good service. They were seated at a table, then she excused herself to got to the bathroom.

In the grungy mirror, she stared at herself, shook her head, and put on lipstick. What was the matter with her anyway? She wouldn't have this problem being in the car with Tom.

She wasn't attracted to Tom, a small voice told her before she could stop it.

She was attracted to Tony.

She washed her hands and dried them on a huge sheet of paper towels, then looked at herself in the mirror again.

How could she be attracted to him? she demanded of the face she saw there. Sparkling eyes and red cheeks didn't lie. She was attracted to him.

All right, she told the image she saw there. You're attracted to him. He's very attractive. Just like Sean. He's a little flirty. Just like Sean. Obviously, you didn't learn your lesson. The only thing you can do now is to get through this without making a fool of yourself again.

Of course, he's *not* Sean, that same little traitorous

voice told her. Tony is a different man. You could give him a chance.

She washed her hands again and put on some more lipstick with a trembling hand.

Then she wiped it off and put on another coat, trying to get it even.

"You're attracted to Tony Rousso," she admitted out loud, "but that doesn't mean that anything has to happen because of it."

Another woman walked into the restroom as she was speaking. She looked at Annie strangely, then disappeared into a stall and closed the door.

Annie sighed and looked at herself one more time before she grabbed her purse and headed out the door.

Tony was sipping a glass of ice water when she returned to the table. He looked up at her as she took her seat across from him.

"I was beginning to wonder if you had found another child to rescue in there," he quipped.

Annie blushed and sipped at her own water.

"It was crowded," she lied, glad that their waitress had returned.

Tony studied her face as she ordered some coffee and a sandwich. She was a beautiful woman. She was smart. She was funny. What had happened to her fiancé?

He was a very up-front kind of guy. It was killing him not to ask her, but he was trying to respect her privacy. Trying to wait her out until she felt comfortable with him. It was painfully obvious that she was far from that point.

Tony ordered a hot sandwich and fries, smiling at the waitress, who smiled back at him. Annie couldn't help but notice that the waitress had a saucy little swing to her hips as she left them.

No doubt hoping that he would notice, she considered with a grimace.

She clenched her fork and pretended an interest in her water glass that it didn't deserve.

"Is your fork dirty?" he asked when they were alone.

Annie looked down at the utensil and shook her head. "No! No, it's fine." She laid it carefully on her napkin.

"Is something wrong?" he asked finally.

"Wrong?" she retorted, looking up at him.

"You seem distracted," he offered his opinion.

Annie searched frantically for some response that didn't involve the fact that she was shocked to find herself attracted to him.

"My parents," she answered after a moment. "They were a little overbearing at lunch today. They have this thing about me being with men. They don't think we can just be friends or working together. They think everything has to have romantic implications."

He shook his head. "Do they feel that way about your partner?"

"No, they know he's married. Tom and his wife

had a baby last year so they feel that's not a problem."

"It's me," he guessed.

She nodded. "Yeah, they know you're single, so we have to be attracted to each other. We can't just be going out to find Sara a home."

"Yeah," he agreed. "My parents are the same. But they want it to be different."

"Well, my parents would too, if you were with the police department," she told him with a small smile.

Tony looked at that smile and thought she looked a little more relaxed. "They have a thing about you only dating in the department?"

"Well, like I told you," she confided, "my whole family is on the force or married to someone on the force. And my ex-fiancé wasn't, so they figure—"

"He was a firefighter?"

"No!" she hastened to reassure him. "He was an accountant, a partner in a big firm on the North Side. But he wasn't on the force, and it didn't work out, so it follows that I need to be with someone who is."

Their meals came and the waitress managed to touch Tony's hand as she poured him another cup of coffee. She smiled and winked at him as she poured him more water.

She might as well sit down and join us, Annie considered, looking away from them to her sandwich.

"Anything else I can get for you?" the waitress asked playfully.

"That's it, thanks," Tony said, seeing Annie look

away. "She's pretty friendly," he said as she left them.

Annie glanced up at him. "Not to me," she told him bluntly.

He decided to ignore the evil look she sent his way. "So, your parents gave you a hard time about going out with me today," he concluded. "And that bothers you?"

"I dated a man from my squad once a few years ago," she explained. "The talk didn't die down for months. Even when the guy was transferred to another part of town. I just don't want that happening with us."

"I can see that," he replied lightly. "I've told everyone that we're working together to find Sara a home. I don't know if that makes any difference."

"I know." She sighed.

"I know," he agreed with a sigh.

"Everyone thinks when you're single that if you spend time with an attractive adult that you must have something going on," she finished.

Tony had been chewing a bite of his sandwich. He stopped and looked at her, then swallowed the rest of the bread quickly and took a sip of coffee. He wasn't a detective but it seemed to him that she had just said that she was attracted to him.

"So," he began, choosing his words carefully, "you . . . uh . . . find me attractive?"

Annie sputtered on a mouthful of water and coughed until tears came to her eyes. Tony obliged by whacking her on the back with his hand, all the time looking into her eyes with a knowing stare that left her unnerved.

"I didn't say that exactly," she hedged, wondering how she could make it right. What was wrong with her anyway? Couldn't she talk anymore without getting herself in trouble?

"What was that you said, Annie?" he asked quietly.

"I said that you were an attractive adult," she explained. "You know. As opposed to being unattractive or a child."

"So I'm not unattractive," he surmised. "But you aren't attracted to me?"

Annie wiped her mouth on her napkin, frowning when she saw that she had wiped off her lipstick.

"I . . . I think you're very attractive, Tony," she replied tightly. "Just like the waitress thought you were very attractive."

Tony glanced at her. Was she a little jealous?

She didn't reveal anything in her pretty blue eyes but she was nervous as a mouse with a cat. He hadn't lived with a household of women not to notice that she'd put on lipstick when she went to the bathroom, then wiped it off again on her napkin.

"But not your type, huh?" he wondered.

"I don't have a type exactly," she told him.

"Just someone on the force."

"That doesn't matter to me," she insisted quickly. "Sean wasn't on the force either."

"What happened to Sean?" he queried, not able to hold it back any longer.

"We disagreed," she answered.

He was surprised that she told him anything, but since she'd started, he wanted to know the whole thing.

"Must have been some disagreement."

"It was," she said, sipping her coffee.

"Must have been more than one," he suggested.

She looked at him levelly. "I don't want to talk about it."

"But your breakup didn't prejudice you against men not on the force," he persisted.

"No," she repeated blandly.

"You just aren't interested in me?"

"I didn't say that," she said desperately. "I just think we should maintain a professional distance while we're working together on this thing."

"So . . . later?"

She stood up quickly. "We should go. We have a long drive."

Tony left a tip for the waitress, then followed Annie to the front door. She insisted on paying for her lunch in such a way that he knew that he had to take it or they would be headed back to the city.

So they split the check and left the restaurant together, not talking.

The sun had gone behind the gathering clouds and Annie shivered as she stepped out of the restaurant.

"I'm sorry," he said when they had reached the pavement.

"It doesn't matter," she told him, stalking away

toward the car, not looking where she was going as she considered their relationship.

Her foot caught a patch of dirty ice and she slid, giving a little cry as she closed her eyes and waited for the inevitable fall to the hard, cold sidewalk.

But she didn't fall. Two strong arms caught her as she was going down and hauled her up against a muscular chest like a limp rag doll.

She opened her eyes and looked into his dark eyes. Their coats were open and they shared their warmth, their breaths frosty in the cold air.

"Thanks," she managed in a soft voice, a fluttery feeling in her chest making her light-headed.

"You're welcome," he insisted, holding her tightly, catching his own breath when he looked into her upturned face.

Their lips were so close that Annie could see the tiny lines that fanned out from the corners of his mouth. He lowered his face still closer, the snow clouds haloing his head.

Annie surrendered to the inevitable. She allowed her eyelids to close and parted her mouth, waiting to taste his lips again.

"You're right," he said, setting her back from him, firmly on her feet. "We'd better get going."

Chapter Five

It started snowing right after they left the restaurant. Heavy wet flakes fell on the car and the road, decreasing visibility as the sky darkened and the clouds gathered. The roads turned slick and the traffic slowed to a crawl down the expressway.

Annie thanked whoever made their crazy weather that day. Anyone could understand not making much conversation when the roads were so bad and the traffic so treacherous. They talked a little about being raised in the city and the possibility of Sara being raised in the country on a farm.

Tony admitted that the idea had appealed to him because he hoped to retire someday and do the same. Get away from the crowds and the noise and the dirty snow and live on the land.

He offered to drive. Annie thanked him but stayed behind the wheel. It gave her the opportunity to think about what was happening to them.

Nothing was supposed to be happening. They were supposed to be working. Nothing more than what would happen between herself and Tom on a shift.

But she had been willing to let him kiss her. Again. When she had sensed that he was going to kiss her, she had waited patiently. She had invited him to kiss her.

In truth, as painful as it was to admit, she had wanted him to kiss her again.

Maybe it was just to compare with the other night. Maybe it was to compare with Sean. She didn't know. But she did know that she had wanted him to kiss her. She had anticipated it, and when it hadn't happened, she had been disappointed and embarrassed.

Had she read him wrong? Maybe he wasn't interested in kissing her. Maybe he was just flirting a little, like the waitress, and he wouldn't go through with anything else.

Goodness knew, he had the perfect chance and hadn't taken it! Maybe he didn't really find her attractive.

She drove toward the farm, talking a little to Tony and torturing herself with reasons why he wouldn't have wanted to kiss her. What did he think of her standing there against him with her eyes closed and her mouth ready for his kiss?

Tony was fighting through his own turmoil. It

wasn't like him not to take advantage of a situation. Especially a situation that he wanted as much he had wanted to kiss her.

He had looked at her lips and he had wanted to touch them so badly that it hurt. They were pink with the cold and turned up at the corners. He remembered how soft they had been beneath his and he had wanted to press her close and kiss her.

Only one thing stopped him. She had said that she wanted to keep their relationship professional. He would certainly be willing to admit that he found her undeniably attractive. But if that wasn't what she wanted, then he wouldn't press her. He had worked with enough women to know how to keep his distance.

"How much farther is it?" she asked as the car continued to plow through snow that was blowing into heavy wet drifts.

Tony looked at the map his brother had drawn for him. "There should be a turn coming up on the right that should take us to the road that fronts the farm," he replied.

"This might be turning into a blizzard," she commented, watching the snow fall on the windshield.

"Let's hope not," he answered grimly. "We're a long way from home if it comes to that."

"You're telling me," she muttered, thinking about how long it could take to clear the roads.

The windshield wipers flapped back and forth, trying to clear the snow, but as fast as they moved, the snow was faster. The window was mostly obscured with heavy white puffs.

They turned down the next road on the right. Annie barely negotiated the slippery turn, the car spinning a little before she righted it and started back down the road.

"That was close," she said, looking at Tony apologetically.

"That was an impressive save," he remarked. "Learn that at the police academy?"

She smiled. "I think I learned that when I first moved out and thought I could save money by not buying snow tires for my car."

He laughed. "That must have been a learning experience."

"It was for the first three or four times I went off the road," she agreed. "Then I broke down and borrowed the money from my father."

"They won't even let me drive the rig to a fire," he said.

"Yeah but you've got that great car," she admired. "I probably couldn't catch it even in the police cruiser."

"Probably not," he admitted. "It's a kit car my uncle put together and gave me for my twenty-first birthday. She can hit one thirty in a straightaway."

Annie grimaced. "I know you're not telling me you've ever taken it out on the street that fast?"

"We took it to Indy last year," he answered calmly. "They let my uncle drive it around the track a few times."

"Sure," she agreed dubiously.

He laughed. "No, it's true."

"I don't see anything out here," she said to change the subject, looking for a farmhouse or some sign that there was habitation out there in the snow.

"This is the right way," he assured her, looking at the map again. He looked out into the early twilight that the weather had brought with it. "I see some light that way."

Annie looked up and agreed. "But where's the drive?"

The snow had blown, mostly obscuring the drive to the lighted farmhouse they could see in the distance. Annie made the turn toward the house where she could see the drive ran off from the road, but the snow was deeper than it appeared. The car ran into a heavy drift at the bottom of the drive and stopped dead.

Annie looked at Tony. "I think we're stuck."

"I'll try pushing," he said, getting out of the car. "You try again."

He pushed, and the tires spun while the engine raced, but the car didn't budge.

"We're stuck," he agreed breathlessly after his exertions. "We'll have to walk up from here. Maybe we can find a way to get the car out after it stops snowing."

The snow was coming down harder and thicker than it had been when they had been on the expressway. Annie locked her car doors and hoped she hadn't turned into a ditch or off the road. The sky was dark with the storm. The horizon was blurred white on white.

Glad that she had worn pants and boots, she trudged along with Tony up the drive. They could see the yellow light from the farmhouse and used it as a beacon to follow so they didn't end up in the field.

"I guess we should have postponed this," Tony said loudly.

"There was no way to know the storm was going to be this bad," she consoled. "The last I heard, we were going to have flurries, not a blizzard."

The wind whipped, blowing stinging snow in their faces, making their steps difficult in the heavy wet snow.

Tony didn't tell her that he had been so eager to see her again that he had jumped at the first opportunity to be alone with her for a while. Looking back on it, it seemed childish. It was something a sixteen-year-old would have done to get the attention of the skinny red-haired girl that she had been.

"My grandparents lived out of the city when I was a kid," he told her. "We used to go out on the weekends and get fresh vegetables and stuff from them. I used to love to go out there."

"What happened to them?" she wondered.

"My grandfather died and my grandmother moved and left the farm to my uncle. He still works it. It's huge. I remember thinking how many houses could have been on that land if it was in the city. My grandmother died a few years ago. I think she always missed the place.''

"It is beautiful out here," she agreed. "In a cold, empty sort of way."

Tony stopped and stared off into the distance.

Annie looked up at him and smiled at the intense look on his face. "You really like this stuff, don't you? You probably even want cows and horses."

He laughed self-consciously. "Maybe even chickens and sheep."

"How does a city boy get to feel like that?"

He shrugged and started walking again. "I don't know. I remember when I was a kid looking at pictures of farms and thinking that's where I'd like to live."

"I never thought about it," she told him. "I thought it was scary to think about what was out of the city. There's not many people and it's so quiet."

"You really are a city girl. Even at heart. I was born in the city but I think the country must be in my blood."

Annie shivered in her heavy coat, feeling snow pack inside her boots. "I'm glad they have their lights on. This could be scary."

"A blizzard is nothing to fool around with," he agreed. "I've done some rescue work in the snow. People get lost when they can't get their bearings. Sometimes they die out in the cold."

"That makes me feel better," she muttered.

He laughed and took her arm. "Well, we have light, so it doesn't matter."

They both looked at the lighted house and to their dismay, the lights faltered and died.

"Great," she said quietly. "I hope your training included finding your way in the dark without a light."

Tony frowned. "I hope so too."

They kept walking, hoping they were going in the right direction. Darkness settled in across the horizon, making the task even more difficult. The snow was white even in the darkness, but so was the sky. It was impossible to tell where they were going.

"See," she started breathlessly, "this is what I like about the city. There's never a place this big with nothing in it."

Tony was holding her hand, trying to make out any objects in the distance. The snow was coming down heavily and the temperature was falling with the darkness. In a short while, they could be hopelessly lost. He remembered hearing stories of people being a few yards from safety, wandering around in the snow and never realizing how close they were to help.

"Cold?" he asked her, moving closer to her when she stepped deeply into a snowdrift.

"Freezing," she commented briefly, trying to keep her teeth from chattering. "These boots are like going barefoot."

"Lean on me," he suggested. "I didn't need to look pretty, so I wore these ugly boots that keep my feet dry."

"Yeah," she said, panting. "It's that guy thing again. No beauty. All brains."

"That's right," he admitted readily. "And dry feet."

"It could be worse," she told him. "I could have worn a skirt."

"Another societal garment placed on women to make them attractive to men," he remarked.

She laughed. "Yeah, not many people think I'm attractive in my uniform."

"I like uniforms," he said, realizing that she was shaking with cold. He wrapped her closer to him to share their warmth. He was prepared to defend the move but she didn't question it. "I think women in uniforms are cute."

Annie wasn't even trying to look up. Her face was frozen with the pelting snow. She concentrated on putting one foot in front of the other.

"Really? I think men in uniform are pretty great too."

"Good thing, since you have to marry a cop," he answered.

"There are other men in uniform," she informed him. "Marines. Security guards. Firemen. Are we going in the right direction?"

He turned her face to the right. "Look."

Not ten feet away was a pale version of the first light they had seen and the outline of a big farmhouse.

"Thank goodness!" she said in some relief. "You could have told me that you saw lights again."

"I can't believe you were letting me lead you blindly through the snow," he said wryly. "You're pretty trusting for a city girl."

Tony knocked on the door and Annie stood beside him, shivering and thinking about how much she did trust him. When it had become difficult to see, she had trusted him to find the way. It was unlike her not to take the lead. Her brothers wouldn't have believed it.

"Hello! Come in! You must be frozen!" The door swung open and the dim light spilled out into the dark, snowy night.

A cheerful middle-aged man greeted them, standing to the side to let them into the house. They huddled in the doorway together while someone was sent to bring towels. Annie was glad just to be out of the bitter cold.

"Oh, I'm so sorry you came all this way in this blizzard," a woman said, coming to meet them. "I'm Angie. This is my husband, Fred. You must be Tony and Annie from the city. Let me see if I can find you something dry to wear. We have some hot soup and a nice fire you can sit beside."

There was a bustle of activity as two older children came with towels. They led Tony and Annie to rooms where they were offered warm, dry clothes.

Annie changed into the older woman's clothing. The shirt and pants were much too large for her but she managed by tucking in the pants with a belt and folding up the sleeves of the shirt. Angie talked to her through the door the whole time and took her back downstairs when she was finished.

Tony was waiting at the fire, already installed in the warmth with a big mug of hot coffee. He was wearing some of Fred's clothes, too large as well, but dry and accommodating.

Annie joined him there and was given a mug of coffee. She smiled at him as a few of the smaller children sat staring at them.

"Are you hungry?" Angie asked. "We have some leftover stew from supper and some homemade bread."

Annie was fine with coffee but Tony ate a big bowl of stew and a huge chunk of buttered bread. They sat beside the fire while Angie worked on her knitting and Fred worked with one of the boys on their homework.

"I don't think there'll be snow tomorrow," Fred said with a smile. "They said this blizzard could be the worst this century but it's already tapering off."

Tony looked at Annie. "Are your phones working?" he wondered. "We'd like to call our families and let them know where we are."

"They should still be up." Angie tried the line. She handed the phone to Annie with a gracious smile. "Here you are. You have such beautiful red hair."

"Thanks." Annie felt self-conscious. She had combed out the red strands she usually kept under her hat so that they would dry. Tony glanced at her over his coffee mug and she tugged at them nervously.

She called home and told her mother that they were snowed in for the night and maybe for the next day.

"Are you with *him*, Anne Katherine O'Malley?" her mother hissed.

Annie grimaced, looking up enough to see that Tony was listening interestedly.

"I'm with Tony and Fred and Angie and their children. I'm all right, Mom."

Her mother had no choice but to accept Annie's word. She urged her daughter to hurry home, then agreed to call the department for her.

Annie said good-bye, then handed the phone to Tony. "My turn to listen."

He shrugged. "I have nothing to hide."

But he spent five minutes on the phone with his mother explaining what had happened and denying her the privilege of talking to Angie and Fred to verify his whereabouts.

"Parents," he said finally when he hung up the phone.

"Wait until it happens to you," Fred told him. "There's nothing else like it."

"You and Annie will make such beautiful babies with the two of you so pretty," Angie told them.

Annie blushed scarlet and Tony smiled.

"Tough cop," he murmured for her ears only, admiring her blush.

"I'm glad you think that's funny," she whispered, then turned to Angie and Fred with a smile. "We aren't married."

Fred and Angie looked at one another. Both of them frowned.

Annie looked at Tony. He shrugged.

''I mean, we're just working together. We found baby Sara together and we're trying to find her a home,'' Annie explained quickly.

Fred smiled with relief and Angie pressed her hand to her heart.

Tony went on to explain that Annie was a police officer and he was with the fire department.

''That's wonderful,'' Angie commended. ''You gave us a fright for a minute.''

Fred nodded. ''Although the two of you could be a couple. There's something about you together. You know, people start to have a look about them when they've been together for a while.''

''You do have that look,'' Angie agreed with a smile.

''But we're embarrassing you,'' Fred remarked with a laugh. ''Sorry. We spend too much time with the children. Speaking of which, let us introduce you to the brood.''

Annie lost track after the first five. She had thought her home was hectic and full when she was growing up. Fred and Angie presided over a veritable army of children. Yet they were all very well mannered and well dressed. The house was immaculate and all the children seemed bright and well cared for.

Here was the home for Sara, Annie thought with a pang. She wished that she could have been the one to provide it for her, but the circumstances didn't allow for it. She would just have to be glad that Fred and Angie were willing to foster Sara.

Tony looked at Annie as she was helping Angie with her yarn. There was everything in the house that could make Sara happy and he wanted it all for her. Yet he wished that he could have been the one to give it to her. He could imagine a home like this of his own. And despite Annie wanting a professional relationship with him and nothing more, he could imagine sharing it with her.

Annie felt Tony's eyes on her as she helped Angie work her yarn into a ball. His gaze made her feel warm and wanted. It was confusing. She looked back at him across the top of a tousled blond head as he was helping one of the children with his reading.

Their eyes met and locked. She smiled at him and he smiled back. They should have looked away then, but their gazes refused to move.

Tony's glance touched her mouth, and her lips parted. Her breath came a little faster. They seemed to be drawn together across the crowded room until there was no one else. Only the two of them together. Only their mouths and their eyes and the touch of their hands.

"Uh . . . Tony?" Fred asked for the third time.

Tony blinked and the room returned, with Fred standing over him trying to get his attention. "Yeah, sorry. I guess I'm tired."

"You'll be bunking up with our oldest, Scott. Annie will be in with Trish. Make yourselves at home.

We should be able to get your car out tomorrow. In the meantime, anything we can get for you, just ask.''

"Thanks. We appreciate it."

Annie nodded. "You've been very kind."

"Nonsense! We love the idea of adopting baby Sara. We're lucky that you came to us," Angie told her. "Now get a good night's sleep and we'll see you in the morning."

There were only three kerosene lamps and they had to be shared between the huge family. They stationed one in the bathroom, up high, so that the smaller children couldn't reach it. Fred and Angie took another and they left one on a shelf near the stairs.

Annie went up the stairs with Trish, who was asking her about Chicago and the malls. She smiled quickly at Tony as he disappeared into a room with the oldest boy, who was plying him with questions about being a fireman.

Tony sketched a brief wave, then the door was closed between them.

Annie lay down in the twin bed beside Trish, listening to the girl's quiet, easy breathing. The house was warm around them, but the wind wailed through the eaves as the cold night blew with the storm.

She got out of bed quietly and went to stand at the window, looking out into the deep night, glad that they weren't out there in the cold and the dark. Happy that Tony had found the house through the snow.

Watching him with the children had melted something inside of her. He was so caring, so patient. He was made to be someone's father. He would have made a wonderful father for little Sara.

And when he had looked at her, she had been willing to agree that she found him attractive, that she wanted more from him than a professional relationship.

It was the moment, she told herself, the warmth and family atmosphere that had attracted her and made him seem so desirable.

Thinking about him made it difficult to sleep. The noises in the old house were unfamiliar. The wind whistled and the furnace thumped. Trish began to snore gently. Annie wrapped one of Angie's robes around the large, flannel nightgown she'd borrowed, then tiptoed downstairs.

Maybe it was the coffee, she considered, that was making her restless and longing for things she couldn't have. Maybe a glass of milk would help. Maybe a cookie.

She sighed. It was going to be a long night.

Coming from the kitchen to the living room with her milk and cookies, she was careful to watch her steps. Darkness pooled in the corners where the lamplight didn't reach. How had people done it a hundred years before when there were no electric lights?

The light from the fireplace was still strong, shedding a warm orange glow across the sofa and chairs. After all the activity of the evening, it seemed odd to see it so empty.

Annie considered, for the first time, what it must be like for her parents with all of their children grown and out of the house at night. From a houseful to an empty nest must be strange, she decided.

A shadow moved in the firelight. Annie was startled and almost dropped the plate of cookies.

Tony caught them.

"What did you do before you met me?" he wondered, handing her back the plate.

"I never dropped anything," she replied. "Or slipped on ice."

"Or went into burning buildings?" he questioned.

"Maybe that's what they mean by when you save someone's life, it becomes yours," she ventured, sitting down near the hearth. "Cookie?"

"No, thanks. You should have had the stew," he whispered, conscious of the sleeping people upstairs.

"It's a wonderful place for Sara, isn't it?" she asked him.

He nodded. "I couldn't ask for any better."

"Fred and Angie seem like great people and their children are wonderful."

"From what I could tell of them," he agreed. "They were a blur there at the end."

"I think Sara will be happy here."

"Who wouldn't be?"

The fire crackled as a log fell in the hearth. The wind whistled downstairs in the quiet. The furnace thumped several more times.

"You couldn't sleep either?" she wondered.

"Scott snores like a jet plane," Tony said with a

smile. "He should talk to you. He wants to be a cop."

"Firefighters don't wear a gun," she told him. "That makes the force very attractive to young men."

"What about young women?" he queried. "What made it attractive to you?"

She thought for a moment while she swallowed her cookie and milk. "I think it was because I always wanted to do what my father and brothers did. I didn't want to play with dolls like my sisters. I wanted to play basketball and ride my bike. I sneaked into my brothers' clubhouse to watch action movies when I was twelve."

"So you're a tomboy?"

"I guess," she admitted with a smile. "Not that I wouldn't like to be married and have children. I just don't like knitting and canning tomatoes as much as running and playing football."

He laughed. "I can imagine you playing football."

"No mercy," she told him firmly. "That's the trick."

She finished her cookies and milk and brushed the crumbs from her hands. It felt too warm, too close, being there with him. She might not be able to sleep upstairs, but she was nervous staying down there with him.

"Well, I guess I'll go back to bed," she told him, standing up with the plate and glass firmly in her hands. "Good night, Tony."

"Good night," he said, standing with her. "Annie?"

She turned to face him.

"You . . . um . . . have a piece of cookie." He stepped closer to her and touched his finger to her chin. His gaze didn't move from hers. He took the small bit of cookie from her chin with the tip of his finger, then touched the tip of his tongue to the cookie bit. "You're right. They are good."

Annie felt her knees grow weak. Warmth flooded through her from her head to her toes. She felt drunk or drugged by the warmth and his nearness.

"Tony," she admitted in a whisper. "I . . . I do find you attractive."

"Ouch," he said, smiling, taking the plate and glass from her and putting them on a small table. "That wasn't easy."

He put his arms around her and she shivered, snuggling her head into his shoulder.

"I guess we're both crazy," she muttered.

He smiled. "I like your nightwear."

Annie laughed. "I like yours too."

He tipped his head back to look at her. "Whatever you say."

Then he kissed her, warm and soft. Yielding what she asked him to yield, giving in a way that made her want to give. His arms were strong and tight around her. If her knees would have given out, she felt sure that he would have caught her. He would never let her fall.

Her lips parted and he answered her, slanting to

cover her mouth with his kiss, reducing her into a melting heap of warm human that only wanted to be closer.

"Annie," he whispered, nibbling at her ear.

"Mmm, Tony," she mumbled, lost in his nearness.

The electricity chose that moment to come back on, revealing two children standing on the stair watching them.

"I think it's time to go to bed," Tony told her, his arm still around her shoulders as they parted rapidly.

Annie smiled, unable to speak, Afraid her voice would tremble at the strength of her emotions for him. She shooed the children back to bed and took her place in her own single bed again, staring at the ceiling, wondering what was happening to her.

Chapter Six

Annie woke with a start the next morning, sitting straight up in bed, wondering where in the world she was. It all flooded back to her. Then she noticed the three pairs of interested eyes watching her from three sides of the bed.

"Good morning," she said hesitantly. "Have I slept too late?"

One small head nodded. "You almost missed breakfast."

She sighed. It was cool in the big room and her blankets were warm. She didn't want to move.

"I'll get up," she said at last when the three faces continued to watch her.

Was that kiss a dream? she wondered, closing herself in the bathroom to get dressed. She had dreamed

92

repeatedly about Tony during the night. Had she really gone downstairs and kissed him?

She looked at herself in the mirror. She looked the same. She touched her lips. It seemed so real. But then so did the other dreams she'd had about him and she *knew* those weren't real.

She brushed her hair and put on a little lipstick. She hadn't slept well until the early-morning hours and it was barely seven o'clock, still dark outside the old windows. Her mind was foggy and she couldn't stop yawning.

The only thing she could do was to wait and see how Tony acted toward her. The kiss seemed real enough, but she didn't want to make a fool of herself.

She went downstairs where the noise and light came from the kitchen area. Her three followers had evidently decided not to wait any longer for their breakfast. They had deserted her for chairs at the table and a steaming bowl of oatmeal.

Annie smiled when she saw it. Oatmeal had been a staple at their house when she had been growing up. Her mother had proclaimed that if it wouldn't have been for oatmeal, they would have starved living on a cop's wages with five children.

She remembered it being served with little faces of brown sugar and raisins. Sometimes, her mother even put chocolate and whipped cream on it. But no matter what, it was always oatmeal for breakfast.

She had complained long and loudly about it when she was a child, but as an adult, she remembered it fondly. It was a part of her childhood as much as the crazy antics of her brothers and sharing clothes with her sisters.

"Good morning," Fred and Angie greeted her simultaneously. "Here we are all together. You can see we nearly have our own football team."

Annie looked down the long wooden table at the shining clean faces of the children who ranged in age from older teens to toddlers.

Tony lounged against the side of the cabinet with his bowl of oatmeal. She felt his eyes on her from across the room.

"This reminds me of my own family," she told Fred and Angie. "We always had at least ten for meals. And always oatmeal for breakfast."

"You are from a big family," Fred said commendingly. "Ours might have come to us from different sources, but we love them all as though they were our own."

"And we'll love little Sara the same," Angie pitched in, coming to stand beside her husband.

Annie nodded, too emotional too speak. She smiled and took a bowl of oatmeal from Fred, then took a seat at the table offered to her by a departing teen.

"Your car looks good and stuck in the drive," Fred told them. "But it stopped snowing. The plow should be here by noon and after that we can pull you out with the tractor and send you back to the city."

"Thanks," Tony replied, shaking the man's hand. "We appreciate your hospitality."

"Nonsense!" Angie said. "We appreciate the gift that you've brought us with little Sara. Thank you."

Tony took a seat opposite Annie as the children finished their breakfast and were sent off to start their chores around the house.

"Sleep well?" he asked quietly while three small children finished their breakfast.

"I was a little restless," she replied. "How about you?"

"Me too," he agreed. "No house makes noises like your own, I guess."

"I guess," she responded with a smile, stirring her oatmeal.

The three last children got up and put their empty bowls in the sink, then left the room. The kitchen was cavernous without all the children. Fred stood by the door, smoking a pipe and trying to wax the runners on an old sled. Angie brought in a dozen eggs from the henhouse.

"I guess I'll get started on these dishes," she stated, looking at the pile in the sink.

Annie glanced up at Tony, then looked away. "Let me help," she offered.

Tony watched her walk to the sink and stand with the older woman. She wielded her dishcloth lightly as they talked about families and running a house with so many people in it.

Was she regretting the kiss they had shared last night? Their conversation had been stilted and uneasy. There had been no furtive smiles and intense glances as he imagined that there might be between them that morning.

He wasn't sure what to make of it. He didn't want to pressure her. Maybe she hadn't meant for it to happen between them. Maybe she was sorry this morning.

And maybe he had an overactive imagination, he considered, giving his bowl and spoon to Angie with a long look at Annie.

He joined Fred, offering to help. They pulled three more sleds out of the big closet and waxed the runners with long flourishes.

"He likes you, you know," Angie whispered to Annie at the sink.

Annie smiled. "Really, we—"

"It doesn't matter if there's anything between you right now," Angie told her. "He'd like there to be something."

Annie glanced at Tony. He was too intent on the sled he was repairing to notice her.

"What makes you think so?"

"The way he looks at you," Angie told her. "There's a gleam in his eyes. I think he'd like to be more than just a work partner."

"Let's try these out," Fred announced after the sleds were ready to go. There was a resounding chorus of approval from the children that had gathered around the two men.

The air was cold, but the sun was warm on their heads and the snow was white and clean, covering everything. The children divided up the five sleds between them and raced out the door, bundled up in their heavy jackets and mittens and boots.

Fred handed Tony a sled and smiled. "Maybe you should take that girl of yours for a ride down the hill."

Tony glanced at Annie across the kitchen. "I don't think she sleds anymore."

"Of course she does," Fred told him. "Every girl likes to be a little breathless from time to time."

Tony looked at Annie again and nodded. She was just finishing up the dishes with Angie. He walked across the room and took her hand, smiling down at her.

"Let's go sledding."

"I'd be all wet," she protested. "We have to go home today."

"We can dry your clothes when you're done, now the power's on," Angie told her. "Go out. Enjoy yourself. Plow's not here yet anyway."

Annie looked at Tony, then past him to the window and the wide blue sky and the dazzling white snow. Recalling her childhood that morning was the only reasonable explanation she had for the thrill of excitement that ran through her.

"Okay. Let's go."

There was a great hill that ran from behind the barn to just before the lake that gleamed in the sun. They trudged together, following the children's happy cries and their footprints in the deep powdery snow.

"I haven't done this in a long time," she said as they walked.

"Neither have I," Tony admitted. "But it's probably like riding a bike. How can you forget how to ride a sled?"

Annie looked at him as he spoke. His cheeks were red with cold and his eyes were dark and laughing. He looked handsome and happy, but he still looked like Tony Rousso. Somehow, she suspected that if that kiss had really happened between them last night, he would look different to her that morning.

They cleared the way between the barn and the house and followed the path that skirted the side of the barn. There was a brief place there where the shadow of the old red barn fell on them and they were screened from both the hill and the house.

Tony looked at Annie with her red cheeks and red lips and he wondered if she was feeling what he was feeling. All night long he had thought about that kiss and wished that there had been more.

"Annie," he started, stopping in the knee-deep snow.

"What's wrong?" she asked, looking up at him.

He didn't even put down the sled. Instead, he caught her close to him with one strong arm and kissed her lightly on her cold lips.

Annie's eyes flew open, then fluttered closed as she rose up on her toes to put her arms around his neck. It hadn't been a dream.

The sun was warm on their heads. Their frosty

breaths mingled in their warmth and they forgot the hill and the children and the sledding.

"I thought I had dreamed this last night," she confessed as he feathered light kisses on the side of her head.

He stopped and looked at her. "I thought maybe you were sorry."

"Sorry? No, Tony, mmmm," she managed to get out before he kissed her lips again.

Long moments passed before either of them were capable of conscious thought.

"We have to talk," Tony said finally, taking her hand and looking down at her with his disturbing intense gaze.

"We do," she agreed.

They both smiled, then Tony kissed her again quickly, their lips lingering, then parting on a sigh.

"First we have to sled," he said firmly.

Refusing to let anything cloud the hazy charm of the morning, Annie held his hand as they walked to the hill.

Tony put the sled down, then sat on the back and held out his arms. Annie sat down on the sled between his long legs. She scooted up close, letting him share his warmth with her. They rocketed down the slippery hill, almost to the lake. Like the children, they ran back up the hill and climbed on again, this time crashing halfway down the hill and rolling breathlessly in the snow.

Annie found herself half lying on top of him, his

arms wrapped around her. He was laughing and she lowered her head and kissed his parted lips.

"My face is numb," she told him.

"We can warm you up," Tony reminded her, rolling her over until he was on top of her, kissing her breathless.

They ran up the hill again and sledded down without incident, but the children were already laughing and nudging each other when they looked at them.

"Kids," Tony exclaimed lightheartedly, snatching a kiss from her again. "They're so immature."

He made a snowball and tossed it at Scott, who promptly returned fire and the battle was on.

The group of children weren't better or faster snowball makers, but there were more of them. Outnumbered and covered with snow, Annie and Tony were retreating when Fred called the children in for lunch.

"It's noon," Annie exclaimed, glancing at her watch.

They ran past the barn with the children. Fred and Angie were waiting by the door, urging them to hurry. Jackets and boots and gloves were all heaped up on the porch, but Angie took Annie and Tony's clothes to be dried right away.

"The snowplow came through while you were down at the hill," Fred told them. "After lunch, we'll go out and get you on your way."

Annie hated to say it, but she wished that the snowplow hadn't come. Being there with Tony was like being a kid and sneaking away from school for the day. It was reckless and irresponsible and she wasn't thinking at all of the future, but she didn't care.

She knew that when they were back in her car heading down the highway, all of that would change. They would be going back to the city and the real world of their jobs and their families and their problems.

They ate peanut butter and jelly sandwiches for lunch with big glasses of frosty milk. It only served to enhance the images of childhood. When the younger children were told to go upstairs for their naps, Annie wished she could go with them.

She looked at Tony, who was yawning too. He smiled at her and she knew that he felt the same.

"I know you two will be wanting to get back," Fred said, standing. "Let's go take a look at that car."

They rode down with the tractor. The snowplow had pushed even more snow up against the car, almost burying it in the heavy white stuff. Scott helped his father attach a chain to a part under the bumper of the car and it only took ten minutes for the tractor to pull the car out.

Annie climbed into the freezing car and tried to start it. The engine turned right over and her heart sank. They were headed back to reality.

"We'll be in touch," Tony promised, climbing into the car beside her.

"We'll talk to our lawyer too," Fred told him over the racing engines of the car and the tractor.

Annie waved, then backed the car out of the drive into the main road where the snow was already melting from the hot sun.

"Nice people," Tony remarked as they drove slowly away from the farm.

"The best," Annie replied. "And they want Sara. What could be better?"

"She'll never want for love or attention," Tony added.

"Or playmates," Annie agreed. "It's a wonderful home."

They drove silently down the interstate for a long time, each lost in their own thoughts. The roads were light on traffic and they made excellent time approaching the city.

About a half hour out, Tony looked at her suddenly.

"What?" Annie asked when he didn't speak, but still sat staring at her.

"What happened? With you and your fiancé? Why did you break up?"

Annie frowned. It wasn't a painful subject anymore but she wasn't sure she wanted to discuss it yet with him.

"It was a disagreement," she replied.

"You said that before," he reminded her.

"Well, that's what caused it," she said, not looking at him.

"What kind of disagreement?" he wondered.

She shrugged. "It was complicated. One of those

moral issues between couples. You know—right or wrong. Good or bad.''

''Moral?'' he frowned. ''You mean it clashed with your being on the force?''

''In a manner of speaking,'' she hedged.

Tony continued to study her averted profile. ''Are we going to try to have some kind of relationship? Or were we just killing time back there?''

Annie looked at him then, and almost ran off the road. The hard crust of snow at the edge of the road pulled at the tires.

She brought the car back under control and looked at the road again.

''I can't talk about this now,'' she told him.

''All right,'' he said. ''Pull over.''

''There's nowhere—''

''There's a truck stop,'' he said, pointing to an exit. ''We can talk there.''

''I'm on duty in two hours,'' she protested. ''Maybe we can talk later.''

''I guess that answers the question,'' Tony said quietly.

Annie glanced at him, then refocused on the road. She tightened her grip on the steering wheel.

''He wanted me to give up being on the force.''

Tony nodded. ''And you weren't willing to do that?''

''Would you give up being a firefighter for someone?'' she demanded.

''It would all depend why, I guess,'' he said thoughtfully. ''Why did he want you to give it up?''

"Because he couldn't stand the strain of not knowing if something was going to happen to me. It happened right after I was shot. He wanted me to be safe behind a desk and let someone else take all the risk."

"So you dumped him."

"I didn't dump him!"

"You let him go," he amended.

"He walked out on me," she stated flatly. "I didn't call him back."

They rode in silence for a few more minutes while Tony digested the information and Annie bit her lip.

"Did you love him?" he asked.

"I thought I did," she answered truthfully.

"But now, you don't think you really did?"

"No. And I don't think he loved me or he wouldn't have asked me to give up something so important to me."

The hum of the tires on the pavement was the only sound as they hit the city limits.

"I was engaged once," he told her softly.

"What happened?" she asked, glad to change the focus of their conversation.

He glanced out of his window, then shrugged. "She didn't want to have any children. She was a trial lawyer and she had a career that didn't include having a family. I wanted children and her. I couldn't have both."

"Then you know what I mean," she added.

"It's not exactly the same," he remarked.

"Basically, when it's not right, it's not right."

"I would've quit the department for her, if it would have made a difference," he explained.

"But she wasn't willing to have children, so it didn't come up."

"Exactly."

"Are you saying if I had really loved Sean, I would have quit the force for him?" she guessed.

"Maybe."

"You didn't give up on the idea of having a family for your fiancée," she reminded him.

"Having a family is an important aspect of life for me," he said. "After losing my mother and being adopted, family means more to me than it does to a lot of people. The department is just a job."

"So you're saying Sean was right to leave me?"

"I'm saying I can understand," he replied gently. "Seeing someone you love put themselves in danger everyday is hard on a person."

"I guess the force isn't just a job to me," she tried to explain. "It's something I wanted for as long as I can remember."

"I understand that too. I've wanted to be a fire-fighter for that long. But I've watched my mother's face when the phone rings and I've seen my dad and my brothers hurt on the job. It's not an easy life for someone outside the field."

"I guess that's why my parents want me to marry a cop," she remarked. "That way, there wouldn't be that problem."

"Have you thought about what you would do if you had a family of your own?" he wondered.

"Would you be willing to go out in the middle of the night to chase drug dealers if you were seven months pregnant?"

She shrugged. "I've known other women who work and have children. There's a risk. There's always a risk. But there's a risk for Sean going into work tomorrow morning and being assaulted on his way."

"I know that argument," he finished. "But we both know the risk increases in our lines of work."

"Does that mean you wouldn't consider marrying someone who had a high-risk job because you want a family?"

He looked away from her. "I don't know."

Annie changed the subject after that and they made plans to meet the next day to talk with Mrs. Jenkins about Sara. She kept her tone light, but her mind was weighed down with his words.

Not that she had imagined marrying Tony Rousso, even in her wildest fantasies. She hadn't known him long enough to fantasize that hard about him. She would always remember that day in the snow and his kisses but she supposed that after they saw Sara safely to Fred and Angie's farm, they would go back to seeing each other when their shifts met.

She dropped him off at his house, declining an invitation to go inside for coffee. She looked at the two-story house with its green shutters and white frame walls.

What was it with men? she wondered. First Sean, then Tony. At least Sean was an accountant and couldn't begin to understand the life. Tony was different. He had lived in a family of firefighters. He knew the risks, but he also knew the obligations of the job. People who stayed for a long time didn't undertake it lightly.

She knew plenty of women on the force who were happily married and had beautiful children. They didn't all work behind a desk or some other safe haven.

Besides, she sniffed, next year she was going to take her exam to be a detective. Everyone knew their jobs were safer. And they were paid better so they could afford a family.

Still, it was depressing to her as she went home and changed into her uniform to go to work.

Tony didn't understand about her job either.

But it was better to find out right away. There was a big difference between exchanging a few kisses and having a good time and thinking about spending the rest of your life with someone. Even when you took your time, sometimes it wasn't the right person.

Would she ever find the right person? she wondered, meeting Tom at the precinct house.

If she did, would he expect her to give up being a police officer?

The night was bitterly cold after the snow. In the city, the white snow had already turned to gray and black slush that froze on the roads as the night got colder.

Tom was having trouble with Alice again. She was threatening to leave him and take their baby if things didn't change. The problem seemed to be that Tom couldn't figure out what to change to make her happy.

"Don't ever get married, Annie," he advised her as they were getting coffee around midnight. "It messes up your whole life."

They answered a handful of calls that night. It was slow because it was too cold for anything much to be going on in the street. Annie looked at the dark silhouettes of the tall buildings as they passed and wondered what was going on inside.

She heard the wail of a fire engine close to 3:00 A.M. and they were called to respond to the scene.

It was an apartment fire that was caused by a faulty electric heater. People just trying to keep warm. The fire department had managed to contain it to three apartments and the Salvation Army was there to help those residents find a place to spend the night.

Annie couldn't help herself. She looked at the fire-fighters in their black uniforms, but Tony wasn't there. She supposed he was sleeping, probably not on duty. One of the firefighters had serious burns on his hands and had to be transported to the hospital. She thought about what Tony had said about being at high risk.

Still, people survived. Her father had been on the force for thirty years and it was probably the same with Tony's father. They had been hurt occasionally, but they had survived. So had their families.

Annie directed traffic along the snowy street away from the fire. She glanced at her watch. It was nearly dawn. Tom signaled her that the area was clear for normal traffic as the fire trucks were packing away their gear and heading away from the apartments.

Annie waved to Tom as he dropped her off in front of the precinct. She was tired, but she had decided to go to the hospital to see Sara. That day or the next, they would probably find out about Fred and Angie being able to foster the baby. After she was moved out to the farm, she probably wouldn't see little Sara again. She wanted to have a few minutes alone with her.

She arrived at the hospital as the sleepy night shift was making its last rounds before turning everything over to the day shift. The floor nurse told her that Sara had finally been moved to a children's ward, an improvement over the baby being kept on an adult floor.

Annie walked down the wide green hallways until she reached the children's ward, then she stopped a nurse to ask about Sara.

"Who?" the nurse asked tiredly.

"A baby girl," Annie explained. "They said she was transferred here. We don't know her real name but they've been calling her Sara."

The nurse checked her charts. "We don't show any baby transfer since last week. Are you sure you have the right hospital?"

Annie retraced her steps, but still couldn't find Sara. The nurses were arguing over what had happened to the baby. Someone called the hospital administrator while Annie was trying to figure out what happened to the baby by questioning the staff.

It was 8:00 A.M. when Tony picked up his phone and heard Annie's voice on the other end.

He listened, half asleep until he heard the panic in her voice and understood what she was saying to him.

"I'll be right there," he told her without another thought.

Chapter Seven

The chaos at the hospital was in full fury by the time Tony arrived. He looked down the corridor and saw Annie standing between two men who looked as though they had just left their beds.

Seeing her in her uniform was a revelation for him. He'd seen her on duty plenty of times, admiring her trim body and pretty face. Yet somehow this was different.

He knew so much more about Annie O'Malley than he ever had before finding Sara. He'd kissed her and held her in his arms. Her smile made his heart pound. Her closeness made his brain turn to tapioca.

When he looked at her that morning, he knew the woman that she was inside the uniform. He saw the determination in her face, the strength and commitment that made her a good officer as well as a good human being. He saw the dedication to her family and to baby Sara, the lengths she would go to make the world a better place, even for one small child who needed her.

He understood what it was about her fiancé asking her to give up her job that made it impossible for her to agree. It wasn't that she ignored the danger or thought that she was invulnerable to it. It was who she was in the uniform and out of it.

At that moment, Tony knew that he wanted both.

Annie saw him and felt a flood of relief. Seeing him made her feel as though it was going to be all right. It didn't make sense. She had been trying to understand why she had called him. Seeing him standing there made it all come together for her.

She excused herself from the two men who were trying to rationalize what had happened to Sara.

He saw her walking toward him and smiled. He couldn't take his eyes off of her. He wanted to reach out, hold her and comfort her, but knew he couldn't. She looked at him and he couldn't speak, couldn't think for a moment.

"What's up?" he asked finally.

"I don't know," she replied, nodding to him as she continued walking, wanting him to walk along, away from the crowd.

He walked beside her until they were out of earshot of the others. "Where's Sara?"

"They can't find her." Despite the uniform to bolster her and her determination not to do it, Annie felt herself allow some of the anxiety that she felt to creep into her face and voice.

Tony saw it at once in her trembling lips and tearful gaze. He took her hand discreetly as they continued to walk down the corridor.

"How do you lose a baby? It's not like she could get up and walk out!"

"Apparently, they thought that she had been transferred to the children's ward but the transfer was messed up. They just aren't sure where they transferred her."

Glad of his support, Annie squeezed his hand gently and didn't let it go.

"Officer O'Malley," one of the men representing the hospital called to her back.

Annie disengaged herself from Tony as she turned back to face them. Tony marveled at the change in her countenance.

"We may have come up with a possible answer," the man continued. He offered Annie a transcript of everything that had happened that day at the hospital.

Annie looked at it, then looked back at the hospital official. "What does this mean?"

He sighed. "It means she could have been transferred to any of the places on that list."

"How do we find out which one?" Tony demanded, jumping into the fray.

The man looked at him. "We'd have to contact each place and send someone to look over every transfer. Obviously they sent her out by a different name. Not that she had a real name."

"Real enough," Annie told him bluntly. "I'll take those."

"Are you going to search for the baby?" the man asked in disbelief.

Annie glanced at Tony. He nodded. "We know what she looks like. It'll be easier for us to find her."

The man looked at her doubtfully as he handed her the rest of the transcripts. "It seems like the police would have something better to do than to find a baby lost in the system."

Annie's eyes narrowed on his face. "I'm off duty, sir. You don't have to worry about your taxes going to pay for me finding Sara. The only thing I have to lose is sleep. Thanks for your help."

Tony stepped into the elevator beside her.

"You don't have to do this," she said as the doors closed.

He consulted his watch. "I'm not on for another four hours. Let's see what we can find."

"Okay," she answered with a smile, glad that he wanted to go along.

He looked at her, seeing the tired lines around her eyes and mouth. "You were pretty tough on that guy back there, O'Malley."

"I know," she yawned. "I'll probably hear about it too."

Tony insisted on driving. He had a fresh night's sleep and she had been up all night. He also insisted on breakfast and coffee before they set out for the first stop on the list.

Annie had been uncharacteristically quiet through

the drive to the restaurant. When they had ordered breakfast and the coffee was poured, Tony studied her tired face.

"You sure you're okay? I can go out on this alone for my four hours, then you can pick up if I don't find her."

"I'm fine," she answered quietly. "I guess I'm just thinking about what happens to kids when they don't have a firefighter and a police officer looking out for them. What would have happened to Sara if we hadn't cared?"

Tony sipped his coffee. It was only experience that kept him from promising her that everything was going to be okay. He wanted to go out and make the world the place she wanted it to be. "She's safe, Annie. Just lost in the system. You make it sound like she's somewhere on the street because they made a mistake. Somebody's going to pick up on it."

"I know," she said. "I know she's safe, just mixed up."

"We'll find her, don't worry," he promised despite his better judgment.

"Sometimes the system gets to me," she told him.

"Sometimes it gets to everyone," he answered. "The trick is not to let it get to you all the time. It works, O'Malley. There's just glitches from time to time."

"I know," she repeated blandly.

When the food arrived, he watched her push her underdone eggs around on the plate and frowned.

"If you don't eat, I'm going to call your captain

and tell him that you're working on an unassigned case.''

Annie looked up at him and smiled. "He wouldn't be surprised.''

He held her gaze across the table. "Okay." He reached out and took her hand in his. "If you don't eat, I'm going to kiss you right here in front of all of these people.''

Annie felt herself warm considerably. "Why would that be so bad?''

Tony felt his pulse race at her saucy reply. "Because these people expect you to keep crime off the street, to protect them from bad guys. They don't expect to see you making out over breakfast.''

"I could arrest you for assault," she proposed. "Maybe that would make them feel better. Set an example.''

Tony grinned. "That probably would keep anyone else from trying anything with you.''

He held on to her hand and leaned across the table, kissing her gently on the lips. His mouth lingered on hers.

Annie opened her eyes, looking at his face so close to hers. She almost forgot they were sitting in a restaurant with a hundred eyes on them.

"If you arrest me now," he whispered to her, "I can probably still make it in for lunch.''

Annie laughed. "But it would make it impossible for me to get a date again.''

Tony smiled and kissed her again. "That works

for me. I don't want you dating strange men anyway."

Annie sobered and withdrew enough to look at him properly. "I won't quit the force for you, Tony."

His dark eyes were intent on hers. "I wouldn't ask you to, Annie."

She smiled, moved her head slightly and kissed him warmly. "In that case, let's eat so we can get out of here."

Tony sighed and sat back in his seat, all thought of food erased from his mind. He watched her eat her breakfast and drink her coffee, glad when some of the normal color came back to her face and her eyes lost that dull glaze.

He cared for her. He couldn't deny it. It scared him and it exhilarated him. What she did for a living scared him too. But being without her was too painful to consider.

When they had eaten and drank a pot of coffee between them, they set out for the first spot on the transfer list.

The staff had been alerted to their coming and took them quickly through the wards to look for Sara. They stressed that they had looked for the baby themselves before their coming and that there had been no sign of her.

Tony and Annie weren't content until they had looked as well, but in the end, the staff was right. There was no sign of little Sara.

The next two spots on the transfer list were the same routine. The staff was faintly annoyed and a little irritated that their competence was being questioned by a uniformed police officer and a tough-looking, dark-haired fireman who didn't mind putting them on the spot.

When the baby wasn't found at either unit, it was as though they had been vindicated. Cleared of losing the baby who meant so much to this pair, they were happy to see them leave.

Traffic was worse by the time they reached the fourth place, a charity hospital, and when they didn't find Sara there, Annie knew she would have to go the rest of the way alone.

She was beginning to feel the strain of having been up for the past sixteen hours but she wasn't going to give up on finding Sara.

"I suppose you should be getting back," she began, trying not to sound depressed or exhausted.

He looked at her. "I'm not giving up that easy."

She watched him pick up his cell phone and dial, then heard him tell the chief that he was taking a personal day. She sighed and leaned her head back against the seat, glad that he wasn't going in to work.

It wasn't that she couldn't do it alone, she reminded herself briskly. It was just much better with him there.

She fell asleep sometime after that without realizing when it happened to her. One minute, she was looking out the window and thinking about Tony. The next, he was touching her shoulder, telling her that they were at the next stop.

"How long have I been asleep?" she asked him, feeling disoriented.

"About forty minutes," he replied, enjoying watching her wake up.

You've got it bad, he told himself. He liked to watch her eat and sleep. It was pathetic.

Annie looked at him. His hand was warm where it rested on her shoulder. He was so handsome with his smiling dark eyes and wickedly curved mouth.

She saw the expression in his eyes change when she didn't move away from him. If it was possible, they were darker, deeper. She lost herself in their depths.

When he kissed her, she put her arms around his neck and pulled him closer. He was warm and strong against her. She felt the muscles in his arms tighten around her and her back arched to bring her against his broad chest.

His kiss made her feel giddy. Lost, until his arms found her. She couldn't think, couldn't bring herself to move away from him. She needed him to be there. Nothing had ever felt so right to her.

Tony kissed her neck, nibbled her ear, and she laughed softly, calling his name, making him shudder against her. He needed her to be closer. He shifted their positions, but there wasn't enough room and it occurred to him that they were in his car. Kissing in his car in front of a medical facility.

They were supposed to be looking for Sara, he reminded himself, then promptly forgot as she tickled his ear with her warm breath. Anything, everything she did made his blood pressure rise.

But they were in his *car!*

A sound caught his attention. It was like someone was knocking on something but he couldn't understand why anyone would be knocking on anything.

Annie kissed him.

The knocking began again, but this time it was like pounding. Was it the engine?

"Tony," Annie whispered.

He kissed her again and recalled that they had to stop. They were in his car.

"Hey! You two in there!" a voice yelled as the pounding continued.

They both looked up from their perspective places in the front seat of Tony's car.

A man stood at the window, looking at them.

"Hey, are you two the fireman and the officer looking for the baby?"

Tony nodded and disentangled himself from Annie's embrace. He sat up and opened the car window. All of the windows were covered in steam.

"Uh . . . yes, we're looking for the baby," Tony said finally.

The man grinned. "You're in luck then. She's here."

Annie bolted upright. "Where?"

"Inside. She's been entertaining us since this morning."

The man walked away and Tony rolled up the window while Annie straightened her clothes and pushed her hair back into place.

"Where are we?" she asked, looking briefly out the window.

"Some nursing home run by the hospital. A woman was transferred here last night for long-term care."

Annie nodded, then glanced at Tony. "Do I look all right?"

His eyes warmed on her face and body as he ran his gaze thoughtfully from the top of her copper-haired head to the tip of her sensibly shoed feet.

"I think you look great."

Annie swallowed hard on a sudden surge of warmth that wanted to send her back into his arms. "Thanks."

He grinned. "My pleasure."

They stepped out of the car. The man from the nursing home had waited for them. He was looking thoughtfully at the car windows. Annie blushed when she saw that they were steamed up from the inside.

Tony glanced at the windows and Annie's face, then stepped forward to offer the man his hand. "Tony Rousso. Chicago Fire Department."

"Frank Howard," the man stated, taking Tony's hand. "I'm the manager here at Shady Oaks."

"Officer Anne O'Malley," Annie introduced herself, feeling awkward. She had been kissing in the car with Tony in her uniform. That had never happened with Sean. She had never lost control that way. Between her emotions for Sara and for Tony, she was beginning to wonder which end was up.

"We've had quite a time with that little one," Frank told them. He held the door open to the red brick building, then waited as Tony and Annie followed him.

"When did she get here?" Annie wondered, looking around them, hating to think of the baby spending one moment there.

"About midnight last night," Frank replied with a chuckle. "I told the ambulance driver that this wasn't the ninety-four-year-old woman on a respirator that we'd been expecting. He said the orders were always right."

"Does this happen often?" Tony wondered.

Frank shrugged. "Nobody's perfect."

The reality of these people caring for a baby for almost twelve hours began to hit Annie. "What did you do about diapers and bottles?"

"We improvised," Frank told her with a laugh. "A woman here still had a bottle from a visit from her grandson. We cut up old sheets for diapers."

"Didn't you try to call the hospital?" Tony asked.

"I tried," Frank answered. "I just couldn't get through until this morning. Then they told me that you would be coming out for the baby."

They walked into an open room, obviously a common area of some sort with a television and a Ping-Pong table. There were a dozen or so lounge chairs and a desk by the window.

But the people, at least a dozen of them, were congregated around the center of the room. Men and women alike were cooing and talking to the star attraction—little Sara in the middle of the table, adoring the attention.

"She's been a delight," Frank told them with a deep smile.

Annie was amazed. "You've done a good job with her."

"It's the closest a lot of these people will get to a child," Frank answered. "She's been the highlight of our year."

Annie swallowed hard on the lump in her throat. Sara squealed with happiness as the men and women gave her their undivided attention. They had made little toys for her from their personal possessions and things they'd found in the kitchen. Then they just sat back to watch her play.

"Does she have to leave right away?" one woman asked, her blue eyes vivid beneath a mop of curling gray hair.

Tony looked at Annie.

"I have to call for a car seat anyway." She shrugged. "We didn't think about that before we set out. But my sister doesn't work too far from here. I'll give her a call."

"It'll be awhile," Tony reported back to the crowd.

"We don't mind," Frank replied with a grin, as smitten with Sara as any of the rest of them.

"Maybe she can stay for lunch," another man suggested.

Annie smiled at Tony. "I'll call."

She called and talked with her sister, who agreed to bring over the car seat but repeated that she needed it back before she could go home that night. Annie explained the situation and her sister was silent for a long moment.

"Aren't you getting in pretty deep on this one, Annie?"

"I don't know what you mean," Annie lied, twisting the phone cord as she spoke.

"You're awfully connected to this baby and Mom told me about the fireman. This isn't like you."

"I know." Annie sighed. "I don't understand it yet myself. Maybe it's my age. Maybe I'm just starting to think about a family and a home of my own."

"Maybe," her sister agreed. "But that baby probably isn't going to be part of that, Annie. You said yourself she's already set up to go to a foster home and be adopted later. Are you doing the same thing with the fireman?"

"What same thing?"

"Personalizing. He saved your life. The two of you saved the baby. Now you're a family who's going to live happily ever after."

"I don't think so." She quelled her sister's urge to play psychologist with her life. "I am attracted to the fireman. I do feel responsible for the baby. But only until she's in the right hands. I don't think I'm fantasizing anything."

"All right!" Her sister gave up. "You're going to do what you want anyway. You always do."

"Thanks for the car seat," Annie said as the line went dead in her hand.

"Your sister giving you a hard time?" Tony asked from behind, startling her.

Annie swung around to face him. "Listening in?"

He nodded, his eyes intent on her face. "How else would I know about the fireman in your life? So, you leading me on or what?"

"My sister thinks I'm leading myself on," she explained. "She thinks I'm fantasizing myself into a relationship with you because you saved my life."

Tony touched her hand, looking down at her fingers splayed out over his. "Is that what this is?" he murmured, coming closer to her. "I'll have to ask her what's making me fantasize myself into a relationship with you then since you didn't save my life."

Annie found it difficult to breathe with him close to her. Her heart fluttered in her chest and she looked up into his eyes to find herself lost in their dark depths.

"My sister always knows what's right for everyone," she supplied as he touched her cheek and made her shiver. "It's her true profession."

"Wow," he said quietly, then kissed the side of her neck, closing his eyes against the sweet onslaught of his senses. "What a great job. Where do I apply?"

Annie felt her own eyes flutter closed as he kissed her forehead lightly. "You don't. It's something you have to be born into."

"I have a sister who was born into it too," he told

her. "Never mind them. Kiss me, Annie. I like this fantasy."

"Me too," she whispered with a smile before she pressed her mouth to his and let the fantasy take her.

"Uh, excuse me, Officer O'Malley," Frank interrupted them with a broad smile on his face.

They came apart slowly, the intensity of the kiss still in their eyes.

"We're going to lunch and taking Sara down. Would the two of you like to come?"

Tony glanced at Annie, who smiled and blushed.

"Of course, thanks," he told the other man.

Frank's smile broadened. "Any time. The two of you make a great couple. Have you thought about getting married and taking baby Sara yourselves?"

"We don't know each other that well," Annie told him quickly.

"I see," Frank said with a nod. "Well, the cafeteria is this way."

"How well do we know each other, O'Malley?" Tony whispered as they followed Frank down the spotless green hall.

"I don't know," she admitted, feeling stupid being caught kissing in the hall like a pair of high school kids.

"That's okay," he replied simply. "We've got time."

They ate lunch in the cafeteria with the residents and Sara. With everyone fighting over who was going to feed the hungry little girl, Annie didn't try to interfere.

Her sister was right about her attachment to the baby. It was going to be hard to get over when Sara was gone.

Tony sat apart from Annie. They had been separated when they had gone up for their tray of lunch and he hadn't pressed the point. After all, they had already been caught twice acting inappropriately, especially Annie, who was still in uniform. He didn't think Frank or the residents of the home would report her, but it wasn't a good habit to get into.

He watched her watching Sara and wondered what she was thinking. She didn't eat any more of the creamed potatoes, creamed spinach, and creamed whatever than he did for lunch. She kept herself away from little Sara as though her sister's words about the baby had struck home.

Tony knew they would have to let Sara go when it was time but that didn't mean that their relationship was a fantasy. He felt something for Annie O'Malley that he had never felt for any woman before. He was hesitant to call it love because he didn't think he had ever been in love before, but it was real and he didn't want to lose it.

The question was, what did Annie feel for him?

After lunch, the baby was tired and wanted Annie to hold her. Annie was flattered that Sara recognized her as a familiar face and held the baby while they waited for her sister.

She heard the disturbance at the far end of the day room where everyone was congregated and assumed it must be her sister with the car seat. She was partially right.

It was the car seat, but her father had brought it.

She saw him looking around the room, thinking that he was looking for her, but when his eyes found Tony's dark head, he made a beeline for the fireman.

Annie clutched the sleeping baby to her and walked as quickly as she could across the room to where Tony stood, talking with Frank, but her father beat her to him.

"You must be Rousso," her father had already begun when Annie reached them.

Tony nodded and stuck out his hand, recognizing Annie's features in the other man's face. "Tony Rousso, sir. Chicago Fire Department."

"Mike O'Malley, Chicago PD. And Annie's father."

"Hi, Dad," Annie greeted him breathlessly.

"This must be little Sara," Mike said, holding out his hands for the baby.

Annie put the baby in her father's experienced hands. Sara didn't stir. She slept peacefully on Mike's shoulder.

"She's a little angel," Mike said quietly, though his sharp blue eyes never left Tony's face. "You've been spending time with my daughter."

"I have," Tony acknowledged.

"I heard you saved her life as well," Mike remarked. "Her mother and I want to thank you for keeping her from reaping the full extent of her stubbornness."

"That's my job, sir," Tony told him. "Your daughter's a fine officer."

"She is," Mike agreed. "Come to dinner tonight."

"I'm on duty," Tony told him,

"Not until 8:00 P.M." Mike apprised him. "I spoke with your chief. He and I used to play poker together."

Tony glanced at Annie's stunned white face. "I'll be there," he told her father, pushing aside his resentment at the older man's high-handedness. His own father would have done the same thing.

"Dad," Annie began to protest.

"You too, Officer. You don't start your next shift until 9:00 P.M." he said, giving the baby back to her. "We'll expect you both around six-thirty."

Annie stared at her father with a worried frown.

"You might want to change that baby's diaper before you make the trip across town," Mike told her, turning back as he reached the door. "She's a little wet. The car seat's by the door."

"Thanks," Annie said, swallowing hard.

Tony stepped beside her. The two of them watched her father walk, straight backed, out of the building.

"How bad can it be?" he asked sarcastically.

Chapter Eight

Annie didn't want to contemplate how bad it could be. Her father and her brothers had done some embarrassing, high-handed things to her before, but this one was the worst. She was tempted not to show up at six-thirty as he commanded.

Imagine, talking to Tony's chief so that he could come to their house and be grilled like a criminal about his life and his involvement with her!

"You're pretty quiet," Tony observed after they had begun their trek across town to the hospital. Annie had successfully managed to get Sara back to sleep in the car seat.

"I'm sorry about my father," she blurted out. "I had no idea."

"I didn't think you set the whole thing up," Tony

confided. He rubbed his jawline where his early-morning attempt at shaving was already leaving a line of dark stubble. "It's pretty much something I'd expect from my family."

"But it wasn't your family," Annie told him. "It was mine. They're so protective. You'd think I was still eighteen."

"Someday, we'll know how they feel," Tony prophesied. "When our kids are grown and we're worried about who they're dating and what they're doing."

"I won't ever be that worried," she promised hotly. "I want my kids to be able to lead their own lives without worrying about me looking over their shoulders."

"He loves you, Annie," Tony said. "If it was my daughter dating me, I'd be worried too."

Annie turned to him. "I told them we weren't dating. That we were just working together."

He glanced at her. "Well, technically that's true. We aren't dating exactly. Just spending a lot of time together."

"Because of Sara," Annie finished.

"Exactly," he agreed.

They pulled into the hospital parking deck.

"Although we weren't kissing because of Sara," he reminded her pointedly.

"That's true," she agreed. "We were kissing because . . ." She faltered.

Tony turned to her after he had parked the car.

"We were kissing because if we had the time, we would be dating."

Annie stared at him. "I guess you're right."

He smiled and kissed her quickly. "Think about it, Annie. I've been attracted to you for a long time. Now that we've spent some time together, I understand why. You are a beautiful, smart, funny, incredible woman. Even when this thing with Sara is over, I want to see you. If you don't feel the same, now would be a good time to tell me."

Annie stared at his strangely familiar face and had to admit that he was right. She didn't know when it had happened, but she knew that she liked kissing him and that she liked being with him.

"I do like you," she admitted truthfully. But the emotions were too new, too confusing for her to tell him everything she was thinking.

"I better get Sara inside," she said to him when she couldn't think of anything else to say. "My car's just around the corner. I'll meet you for dinner, I guess. Not that you have to come. My father is so—"

Tony kissed her hard on the mouth and interrupted her apologetic speech. "I'll be there, Annie."

Annie took the baby into the hospital, and the head nurse for the children's floor greeted her.

"We're sorry for the mix-up, Officer O'Malley. It won't happen again while the baby is in our care."

"Thanks," Annie said, giving Sara to her.

Sara cried and looked at Annie with her arms outstretched, her little face crumpling as the nurse took her away.

Annie turned away before she went after the nurse and asked her to give the baby back to her. She had to remember, as much as she was attached to Sara, she wasn't her baby.

Leaving Sara crying and reaching for her was one of the hardest things she had ever done. It was just as well that Fred and Angie were going to take the baby soon, she considered on her way back to her car. It wasn't good for her to get any closer to Sara.

Annie returned the car seat to the office where her sister worked, refusing to look at her sister's smug face when she knew that she had called her father into the scene to deal with Annie's fantasy.

She would see her soon enough anyway. There was no doubt that everyone in her family would be there for dinner that night to meet and dismember Tony Rousso.

She didn't bother going home. She stopped at a little dress shop down the street from her apartment where she had been admiring a sapphire blue dress that she was going to splurge on for dinner that night. She needed all the help she could get.

While she showered and dressed, her weary brain went over everything that had happened between them since she met Tony.

With breathless honesty, Tony had admitted how he felt about her and that he would like to further their relationship.

Annie would have liked to have returned the honesty, but her emotions were still raw from her fiancé's desertion. Everything had seemed to be going well between them too, until she had been shot and Sean had hastily backed out of their relationship.

Tony said he understood about her not giving up her job, but she wasn't sure she could trust her heart anymore. It had lied to her once about Sean being the right person. Suppose it was lying again?

Because there was no doubt that Annie felt something frightening in intensity for Tony. He looked at her and she crumbled. When he put his arms around her, she didn't want him to ever let go. She hadn't known Tony as long as she had known Sean, but her heart was already pumping hard when he was near. Just seeing his face made her smile.

She looked at herself in the plain but elegantly cut blue dress. She'd put up her hair and for once, it was staying in place. She had used just the right amount of eye shadow and lipstick, but the glow on her cheeks and in her eyes had nothing to do with makeup. She put her hands to her face and looked hard and long at herself in the mirror, not believing what she was seeing.

She was in love with Tony Rousso. It was plain and simple. And she was terrified by the prospect.

When she arrived at her parents' house, the light was blazing from inside while ten cars were parked outside on the brown grass and in the street.

She'd been right. Only a few phone calls had brought all the members of her family home for dinner that night. Meet Annie's fireman, she could imagine her mother saying to her brothers and sisters.

Tony was already there. She had to give him points

for bravery. First, he saved her and Sara, then he admitted to his feelings for her without any support from her. Then he went into her parents' house without her. The man was a born hero.

Setting out to save him, she walked boldly into the house. It was warm and smelled of fresh bread and something sweet in the oven. Children were running and crying through the lighted rooms. The television set was loud with some sports game that she knew her brothers and her father would be watching.

"Where is he?" she greeted her sister as she turned the corner into the kitchen.

"Hi!" Her sister mocked her. "Nice to see you too."

Annie looked beyond her sister, into the kitchen, but only her mother and two sisters-in-law with their babies were there.

Two of her cousins were on the stairs playing with little cars and dinosaurs. The hall was clear and the dining room was empty except for a huge spray of red roses and ferns that she guessed must have come from Tony. None of her brothers ever brought flowers, except on Mother's Day.

She knocked on the downstairs bathroom door, but there was only one of her brother's children trying to flush the toilet as many times as he could.

Where was Tony?

Annie heard a shout from the den and gravitated that way. She stood at the doorway, watching in wonder, as Tony and Patrick jumped up at the same time and slapped each other's hands while her father roared for victory.

"They did it!!"

"I can't believe it!!"

"Championship! We're talking championship!" Patrick yelled, laughing and dancing around the room.

Two of her other brothers sunk down in their chairs. Obviously, they weren't rooting for the same team.

"Tony?" Annie called when they had reduced their enthusiasm to quiet exultation.

He looked up across the room at her and she smiled. It stunned him to see her again. She was so beautiful. He might not be sure what love was, but if that wasn't it, he didn't want to know. He only knew that he wanted to be with her and wanted her to be with him.

"The boss is calling," Mike O'Malley told him. "Marry her, Tony. It's the only way to get any peace."

Tony grinned and left them to the television, sliding an arm around Annie's waist as they walked out of the room together.

"You look great," he said when they were in a quiet corner of the long hallway.

"Thanks," she replied quickly, feeling his other arm come around her as well. "They like you, don't they?"

"We have mutual interests," he told her with a smile.

She shook her head. "I can't believe it."

Tony frowned and pulled her close. "Am I that hard to get along with?"

"No, but my family is that hard to get along with," she answered truthfully, wanting to tell him what she was feeling for him. Wanting to be as brave as he was with her.

His eyes gleamed wickedly. "Your lipstick is perfect. I hate to mess it up."

Annie's lips parted and she smiled. "I can always put it on again."

He kissed her, almost pulling her up off her feet. She wrapped her arms around his neck and clung to him, not thinking about the audience they could be gathering or the exquisite moments that were passing.

"Dinner!" her mother yelled from the kitchen.

Annie looked up to find her cousins and two of her sisters standing in the hall beside them, watching them kiss.

"Dinner," Mike said as he passed the two in the hall. He winked at his daughter. "You can't live on love, little girl. He's a man and he's on duty later."

Annie sat down at the long, scarred wood table that had seen them through thirty years of marriage, a host of children, grandchildren, aunts, cousins, and usually a police officer or two.

She felt as though she must be in a fairy tale. Her family never liked or accepted Sean. Sometimes, she blamed their breakup on her family, it had been so bad. Most of the time, she knew that they just hadn't been right for each other.

But there she was, sitting beside a handsome man who wasn't a policeman, having dinner with her loud, overbearing family who liked her partner.

Even better, she was sitting beside the man she loved. Maybe he even loved her. He had said that he wanted their relationship to continue. If he didn't actually love her now, maybe he would after they had been together for a while.

It was like a dream.

A rudely interrupted dream when the pagers most of them carried went off at almost the same time.

"Must be big," Mike said, looking at his oldest son.

Tony's pager went off as well and they looked at him thoughtfully. "A fire."

"A big fire," Patrick added.

Dinner was quickly forgotten as husbands, brothers, fathers, and sons arose from the table and said their good-byes.

There was always a feeling that it might be the last good-bye, with a trace of fear lingering in the kisses they exchanged and the final glances that followed them from the room.

"I'll keep dinner hot, Mike," Annie's mother told her father as she had done every time he walked out the door for thirty years.

"I'll be hungry when I get back," he replied in the same way that always separated them.

Annie had grown up with it, but she had never really grown used to it—seeing her mother's and then her sisters' faces as the men left the room.

Sometimes, she thought those faces and the unspoken fear might have been what had caused her to become a police officer. She got up quickly and left with the men.

At the doorstep, Tony caught up with her. He kissed her hard and fast. "Be careful. You haven't had much sleep."

"I will," she replied, dazzled by the light in his dark eyes. "You too."

He turned to go and she tugged at his sleeve. "Will you come back? When it's over. We could still have dinner."

Tony smiled down at her. "I'll be back, Annie."

Annie watched him jump into his car before she ran to change her clothes.

If she married him, she realized that she was going to be caught between the two worlds. She herself might be getting up and leaving for a dangerous assignment, but she was going to be wondering if he would come back alive and unhurt as well.

It only took her a few moments to change into the uniform that she kept at her parents' house in case of emergency. Her mother knocked at the door as she was starting to pin her hair up under her hat.

"Be careful," her mother admonished.

"I will," Annie told her.

Her mother studied her face. "I like Tony. He's a good man. I can see it in his eyes."

Annie smiled and hugged her mother impulsively. "I like him too, Mom. I have to go."

"Come back for dinner," her mother yelled after her as Annie took the stairs two at a time.

"I will," her daughter answered, slamming the door shut on the cold night air.

The fire was in the office district downtown. Units from as far away as the suburbs had been called in to help battle the blaze that was threatening half the skyline along the lake. It had spread alarmingly fast, lighting the night sky ominously.

Police had been called in for crowd control and to keep traffic away from downtown. The roads leading to the heaviest traffic areas in the city were strangely empty as Tom and Annie's cruiser crept down to the site of the fire's beginning.

"These buildings are supposed to be fireproof," Tom complained as they saw the fire raging inside of the multitowered building. "Where's the contractor at a time like this?"

He and Annie were assigned to keep the crowd away from the dangerous area. The crowd had grown steadily in proportion to the fire. The orange flames from the skyscraper reflected in their faces as they pushed closer to get a good look.

Annie pushed her hat back on her head and pushed back when the crowd surged forward. An explosion from behind her rocked the area and sent a shower of glass out toward the street, hitting a few people in the crowd.

"Call for medics, Tom," she yelled above the noise of the astonished crowd.

"I'm calling for backup too," he shouted back at

her. "There's too many of them. We need to move them back farther in the street."

Annie agreed and started moving the front line back. They needed room for the fire trucks as well as the medics when they arrived. Judging by the size and strength of the fire, it was going to be a long night.

Another division sent in trucks and men to contain the fire. Annie's eyes fell on Tony in his dark, protective gear as he left the trucks and went toward the building.

He hadn't seen her, she thought. Or he hadn't wanted to give any sign. The roar of the fire and the water from the heavy hoses would have kept them from doing anything but shouting at one another.

She continued to push back the unruly crowd, trying to get a glimpse of Tony, praying that he wouldn't have to go into that inferno. More officers arrived along with medics from the hospital.

She caught sight of her father standing at a barricade with several department heads, trying to decide what should be done to contain the disaster. She had already seen her brother Patrick working the crowd lines on the other side of the second building that was on fire.

The crowd began to move back, like a tide of living beings, receding as the medics arrived to help the injured.

In a brief flash, Annie saw Tony and several other firefighters enter the building. Her heart was in her throat as she realized the danger he was in.

All she could think about were the words she hadn't said to him. She had wanted to tell him that she loved him. She had wanted to match his spirit and his bravery in their relationship.

But the words had failed her. She might never get another chance to tell him how she felt.

People in the crowd protested at being asked to move back. Reporters and photographers vied for places, trying to talk to her and take pictures at the same time.

All Annie could hear was the roar of the fire behind her. All she could see was Tony's face when he had told her good-bye at the house. She was terrified for him. The professional in her that always understood, always kept it under control, was gone. In her place was the same little girl who used to be afraid when her daddy went to work.

It occurred to her that she had done Sean an injustice when he had asked her to give up the force. She had thought that he was unreasonable, but faced with a similar situation, she was forced to acknowledge that she was afraid as well.

How had her mother lived her whole life waiting and wondering what was happening to her father when he went out to work?

Another blast shook the city street. Glass and masonry flew in all directions. People panicked and ran, running over slower people around them in their attempt to get away from the destruction.

Annie turned back to face the building in time to

see half of the top stories slide into a heap of twisted metal, glass, and concrete down into the foundation.

She yelled out Tony's name. She couldn't stop herself, although it was impossible to hear a single scream above the noise of the fire and the crowd.

If he had been in the building . . . Annie shuddered, trying not to speculate.

She couldn't leave her position, but she searched the crowd for his face and form, hoping a fireman would come by and she could ask him if he had seen Tony.

Medics made their way through to find the injured in the crowd and her radio squawked a message that they were going to have to clear the street any way possible. The risk to the onlookers had become too great.

A helicopter flew low overhead and screamed a warning that the street would have to be cleared. Annie kept her part of the crowd moving backward. It had become easier after the last blast. Helicopters were joining the fight against the fire as well. Huge sprays of chemicals were being dropped on the main fire while the firefighters tried to keep the fire from spreading.

Please let him be all right, Annie prayed for Tony while she did her job. *Please don't let him be hurt. Let me be able to tell him that I love him.*

She imagined her mother and sisters watching the fire on the news at home, praying the same thing for them. But while they were out on the street, they weren't in the middle of the inferno.

Tony had to run out before the last explosion, she comforted herself. He was probably standing on the sidelines with the other men that had entered the building. They had all come out before the blast had virtually leveled the building.

But in the back of her mind were the pictures she had seen before on the news of them taking firefighters out after a bad accident. She had seen fellow officers shot in the street and it hadn't scared her as much.

They were always careful, she reminded herself. They didn't take unnecessary chances.

Two other uniformed officers were sent to help her control the crowd. Scared by the force of the fire, the people who had wanted to see what happened were moving away of their own volition. Still, Annie couldn't leave her position.

"There's two firefighters down in that last blast," a voice squawked over her radio. "They're trapped in the building."

Two! Annie had seen three go into the building. Was Tony trapped or had he made it out?

The crowd had begun to disperse even as another blast echoed across the lake and down the dark streets. The rest of the building slid down until there was nothing but a flaming heap of debris left. If there was anyone trapped in the foundation now, they wouldn't be getting out.

Annie couldn't stand it anymore. "Cover for me," she shouted to one of the other officers.

"Where you goin'?" he yelled back at her.

She didn't stop to answer. If she was called for it later, that would be later, and she would know what had happened to Tony.

She ran through the bulk of the firefighters and police force as they helplessly watched the building fire burn itself out. At least there was no longer a risk to the other buildings around it.

Annie looked for the numbers on the trucks and finally found Tony's division. The firefighters were still hosing down the building as close as they could get to it. It was difficult to tell who was there with the equipment and the smoke in the eerie orange darkness.

"Tony?" she yelled to one firefighter who was treating other firefighters for smoke inhalation. "Tony Rousso! Have you seen him?"

"No," the first one called back. "Try the command post." He pointed to a large group of equipment and personnel.

Annie continued to run, dodging pieces of cement and steel that had flown out from the building and were littering the street. She searched frantically for any sign of Tony, stopping a few men who looked like him.

When she reached the command post, her father was there with the other captains and several fire chiefs.

"Dad!" She hailed him through the group.

Mike O'Malley waved her through to his side. "What are you doing here? I thought you were on crowd control down the street?"

"I was," she agreed breathlessly. "I saw Tony go into the building before the last explosion. Is he okay?"

Her father turned to confer with one of the fire chiefs, then he turned back to her. "They don't know. Four firefighters went into the building. Two came out just after the blast. They were taken to county hospital. The other two are still down there."

"They don't know which two?" Annie asked wretchedly, hating to ask someone to make the distinction, knowing there were other families who would want their husbands and children to be safe.

"Not yet," her father told her. "When I find out, I'll let you know. Get back to your position."

Annie started back. She had her orders and she meant to follow them. But the crowd had been dispersed or contained and the street was clear. She had never disobeyed a direct order in her career, but she found herself in her squad car, ready to leave the scene.

"Where are you going?" Tom demanded, reaching her side.

Annie frowned. "Better go back, Tom. I'm going to the hospital."

"It's the fireman, isn't it?" he asked with a small smile playing on his face.

She turned to him. "I have to know if he's okay."

"All right." He climbed into the passenger seat.

"What are you doing? I'll probably be demoted for leaving the scene," she told him.

''Not if you're taking your partner in for emergency medical treatment,'' he said quietly.

She stared at him, then smiled and shut the car door. ''Thanks, Tom.

''What are partners for?''

Chapter Nine

County hospital was overflowing with firefighters and injured police officers. Between them were people who had been in the crowd at the fire, as well as casualties of other accidents in the night.

It was almost midnight, but the hospital was at full throttle trying to cope with the onslaught. Normally, they would have been busy. That night was impossible.

Annie looked for her sister-in-law, hoping she could help her with some information. She had helped Tom into the emergency room and he had claimed that his eyes were burning and he was having difficulty seeing.

It was hard to believe Tom had bent the rules for her. It wasn't like him. Or perhaps she had misjudged him as she had misjudged Sean. It was a night of revelation.

But please don't let it be at the expense of Tony's life, she prayed.

She finally spotted her sister-in-law, hurrying down the wide hall with a patient.

"Eileen," Annie called and was rewarded when she slowed her frantic pace.

"Are you hurt?" Eileen asked.

"No, I'm looking for Tony. Have you seen him brought in?"

"The fireman?" Eileen asked, thinking back to what she had seen and heard.

"You talkin' about Rousso?" the man in the wheelchair cradling a bandaged arm asked them.

Both women looked at him.

"Yes," Annie stated. "Have you seen him?"

"He was brought in a few minutes before me with Kowalski. They were both in the building."

"Thanks," Annie thanked both the man and her sister-in-law with a smile. Then she was gone. Her hands were cold and her head hurt. He had to be all right. If he made it to the hospital, he had a better chance.

The front desk was busy with intake and nurses running back and forth. Annie bit her lip, contemplating using the uniform she wore as a way to gain information ahead of the other people who were waiting.

She never used it, she argued with her conscience.

What would it hurt just this once to find out about Tony?

"Officer?"

She swung around and faced the doctor who had hailed her. Her hair had come loose as she had been running. A bright curtain of it swung into her face. She pushed it back with a gloved hand.

"Yes?"

The young man smiled. "Are you Officer O'Malley?"

"Yes, I am," she answered, trying to sound calm. "Is there a problem?"

"My patient insisted that I look for a beautiful, red-haired police officer in the waiting area before we work on him. You're the only one who fits that description."

"Tony?" she asked, holding her breath.

The doctor consulted his chart. "Anthony Rousso. Yeah, that's him."

"How is he?" she asked as he started back toward the examining room and she walked along beside him.

"He's in pretty good shape for a man who had a building fall on him. Some lacerations that need a few stitches. Might be a concussion. We think his arm might be fractured, but we can't tell until we x-ray and he wouldn't go up until we found you."

Annie breathed a silent prayer of thanks. Her body felt limp with relief. "I appreciate you finding me, Doctor."

"No problem," he said, opening the door. "Okay,

I found her. You have five minutes, then we're taking you upstairs even if I have to sedate you.''

The doctor smiled at Annie, then left the two of them alone.

''Annie?'' Tony called, trying to see her face around the curtain that was pulled to shield the bed.

''Tony,'' she answered, walking quickly to his side and taking his hand in hers.

His face was streaked with dirt and his uniform was torn in several places, but he was alive and, for the most part, uninjured. She closed her eyes and took a deep breath, hoping that he couldn't feel the way her hands were trembling.

Tony smiled and put his head back against the bed. ''I knew you'd be here.''

''I was so worried. I left my position in the street when they said you were at the hospital.''

He frowned. ''You shouldn't have done that, Annie. You'll probably be reprimanded.''

''I wouldn't have cared,'' she told him bluntly, holding tightly to his hand. ''But as it turns out, my partner broke a few regs and covered for me.''

Tony laughed. ''Be careful, Annie. He might have noticed that there could be something between you after all.''

''He was just helping me out,'' she scoffed.

''Right.''

''Not every man who knows me wants to throw himself at my feet,'' she explained mildly.

''Just me, I guess,'' he said quietly, his eyes closing for a moment.

"Tony?" she called, feeling her heart bump at his words. "Are you all right?"

He looked at her. "Just tired. I feel, well, I feel like a building fell on me."

"Should I call the doctor?" she asked, concerned for him.

"I'm okay," he replied, reaching across to take her other hand in his. "I needed to see you."

"All right. That's it," the doctor told them, reentering the room. "We need to get you up to X ray."

Tony closed his eyes again. "All right. Let's go."

"You'll excuse us, Officer O'Malley?" the doctor asked, calling in two orderlies to take Tony to the X ray.

Annie nodded as they wheeled the bed out of the room. "Can I wait for him to come back?" she wondered.

"It could be awhile," the doctor said with a sigh. "We're pretty crowded."

"I know," she answered. "If you could have someone tell me when he's back?"

"Sure." He patted her shoulder. "He's going to be fine, though. You look beat yourself. There's coffee at the front desk."

Annie nodded and watched them take Tony to the elevator. She walked back to the waiting area that was flooded with people wanting information about their loved ones. Children were crying and the wail of ambulances pierced the night like a knife.

Annie was exhausted. The adrenaline that had propelled her through the street and the night to find

Tony, had worn away leaving her feeling limp and strained.

Tony was all right. That was the important thing. Her heart sang with the knowledge and the warm look in his eyes when he had told her that he needed to see her. He might have been joking about throwing himself at her feet but she didn't care. It was enough that he had held her hands.

She realized that she had missed another opportunity to tell him that she loved him. But she had been so glad to see him, so relieved that he wasn't seriously injured, that everything else had fled before her emotions.

I'll tell him when he comes back down, she promised herself with a yawn. Then she curled her legs under her and promptly fell asleep.

The next thing she knew, Eileen was shaking her awake, calling her name.

"Tony?" she asked, half asleep.

"He's back," Eileen told her. "He's in a room upstairs for the night."

Annie stretched as she stood up, trying to work the kinks out of her back after sleeping on the hard chair. "What time is it?"

"A little after 3:00 A.M.," her sister-in-law said. "Coffee?"

"After I wash my face," Annie said gratefully. "Do you have a comb I can use?"

Eileen showed Annie the bathroom and found her a patient care package that had a comb and some soap and mouthwash.

Annie looked at her blanched face in the mirror with the terrible fluorescent lights above her and flinched. Tony was going to be terrified to see that freckled white face!

She washed her face and combed her hair, securing it back from her face with a loose band. Then she swished with mouthwash and pinched her cheeks. The effect was much better. She was a little less frightening.

There wasn't much left of the night. Eileen had told her that he would probably be released in the morning after a night of observation. He had been lucky and escaped a fracture though his arm was badly bruised. The doctor just wanted to be assured that he was all right after the terrible accident.

Annie crept up the halls through the hospital that was finally quiet. Sometime during the three hours she had slept, the injured had been put in order and the hospital had resumed its nightly routine.

She thought about Sara, asleep in the children's ward, dreaming baby dreams about bottles and soft hands. In a few days, she would be at Fred and Angie's home, enjoying her new life with her new brothers and sisters. She wouldn't remember the two who had saved her and had worked so hard to find her a decent life.

She reached the floor where Eileen had told her that they had taken Tony. The nurse glanced at her as she walked by, but didn't speak. Down the hall, the janitor was waxing the green floor with a back-and-forth motion of his machine. It made her feel as though everything was all right. Someone had it all in hand.

Tony was sleeping as she pushed open the door to his room. She pulled up a heavy green chair and sat beside his bed. He didn't wake up when she touched his hand.

He looked so young and vulnerable. His dark hair was tousled and a lock hung down in his eyes. Someone had washed his face and changed his clothes into the sterile green hospital gear. His injured arm was bandaged, the white very pristine against the dark green blanket that covered him.

There were a few scratches on his face and a cut near his mouth. Annie longed to reach up and touch his hair and his cheek, but didn't move for fear of waking him.

So many thoughts and emotions spun through her brain. She felt as though her eyes had been opened to Sean's fear for her. All the years she didn't understand her mother's weakness, watching her father leave for the job with tears in her eyes.

Now here she was, fighting back her own fear and guilt, wanting to cry. Only the uniform kept her together. She represented the city. People trusted her, depended on her to hold it together, even when everything else was falling apart. She wouldn't let herself or them down now.

But it gnawed at her. She stared past Tony into the dark night beyond the window and wondered if she could handle being in love with a man whose job was synonymous with danger, who saved other people at the possible expense of his own life.

She knew her own job was much the same. How many of the young men and women who had started with her out of the academy were dead now? How many had quit because it was too dangerous?

She had never really considered it before. It just went with the job. Coming from a family of police officers, it was a fact of life.

Tony stirred, sighing in his sleep. His grip on her hand tightened and he opened his eyes to look at her.

"Are you still here?" he asked in a deep whisper.

"I guess so," she replied, leaning closer to him. "How do you feel? Do you need anything?"

"Just this," he answered before he used his good hand to draw her near enough to kiss.

Their lips met and clung. Annie twisted closer to aid the contact. While he was kissing her, she didn't think about what had happened or how afraid she had been. She could feel his warmth and his strength. His lips were real against hers, asking for more, his hand bringing her closer until she was half-lying across the bed.

There was so much more that he wanted than the hospital bed or his injured arm would allow. But whatever he could have of her that moment, Tony wanted it. She was sweet and warm against him, soft and loving with her gentle hands and angel kisses. Her gun pressed into his side, but he ignored it. He tried to use his injured arm and grunted at the pain the effort cost him, but he still didn't let her go.

There was a knock on the closed door and Annie's eyes popped open. "I think we have company," she said to him.

"Tell them to go away," he retorted, not making a move to release her.

"Tony? Are you in there, son?" a voice called from behind the door. "The door is locked."

"I think it's your father," Annie persisted, starting to draw away from him.

Tony groaned. "I'm injured," he whispered, trying to keep her close. "One more kiss."

Annie couldn't resist him. She kissed him once more. Their lips met and clung, then parted. Tony groaned and Annie met his lips again, their mouths fusing hotly against one another.

"Tony?" a woman's voice called from behind the door. "Tony, are you in there? Are you decent?"

Annie moved away from Tony, her hand covering her mouth. "I think that might be your mother."

"I think you're right," he agreed, not letting go of her. "Don't leave. Stay and meet them."

"All right," she agreed, trying to get her shirt tucked back into her pants. She straightened her hair and glanced at herself in the mirror over the sink to see her swollen lips and bright eyes.

"You look beautiful," Tony told her, watching her as she tried to make herself presentable.

"Thanks," she quipped, "but I was hoping for professional."

She opened the door and smiled at Tony's parents.

"Sorry. I guess the door is broken or something. It must have locked when I closed it."

"You must be Annie," Tony's mother stepped forward, assessing the other woman silently. "I'm Sandy."

"Officer Anne O'Malley," she introduced herself, extending her hand to them both.

Tony's father nodded. "I'm Angelo Rousso. How's he doing?"

"He's in pretty good shape for somebody that had a building fall on him," she repeated. "I think he was pretty lucky."

"They told us he'd be coming home today," Sandy Rousso explained. "He's going to stay with us for a few days."

"That would be good," Annie agreed.

"You're welcome to visit," Tony's father invited. "I'm sure he wouldn't have it any other way."

"Thanks," Annie added. "I appreciate the offer."

"Excuse me," Tony said above their quiet conversation. "I have a few bruises and some stitches. My hearing is still good. Could you stop discussing me like I'm not here?"

Sandy Rousso rolled her eyes at Annie. "He always gets so cranky when he's sick."

"I'm not sick, Mom," Tony protested. "And I can go home and take care of myself."

"He's a man, Sandy," Angelo told his wife. "He doesn't need you to fuss over him."

"He's my son. I'll fuss over him."

Angelo threw up his hands and shook his shaggy gray head.

"How did it happen?" he asked his son.

Annie took a chair by the door, but sometime after the start of their conversation, she fell asleep with her chin resting in her hand.

"She's exhausted, poor thing," Sandy said when they noticed that she was asleep.

"She needs to go home and get some sleep," Angelo stated flatly. "She can't do anything else for you here, other than the obvious, and I think that can wait."

Annie woke suddenly, realizing that the room had gone quiet and that everyone was staring at her.

"Go home," Tony told her gently. "You didn't get any sleep yesterday between shifts and you've been here all night. I wish I could drive you. I hate for you to drive home this tired."

"I'll be fine," Annie told him. "Don't worry. I'll talk to you later."

"That's stupid," Sandy told her. "I'm not leaving yet. Angelo can take you home and come back for me. No problem. But come to dinner, Annie. Everyone wants to meet you."

"Oh no," Annie protested, looking for someone else to back her up. "That's too much trouble. I'll be fine."

But she was outnumbered. Tony and Angelo agreed with Sandy and before Annie could come up with a good reason why it shouldn't happen, she was already in Angelo's car, riding down the street.

"Tony always did have a hard head," Angelo told her with a grin. "I could have saved them the money to x-ray that skull of his."

"He's pretty stubborn," Annie agreed with a polite smile.

"When he was ten years old, there was a pear tree in the backyard. I told him, don't climb the tree, you'll fall. What did he do? He climbed the tree and boom! Fell on his head. I look out the next day, he's in the tree again. He falls again. Boom! I finally had to cut down the tree to keep him from killing himself."

Annie smiled and thought about the embarrassing things that her father and brothers had told Tony about her while they were watching football.

"So everyone in your family is on the force?" Angelo continued, keeping his eyes on the road.

"Almost," she replied. "I'm the only woman with a shield."

Angelo glanced at her. "That could be bad for kids, huh? A pregnant cop?"

Annie smiled harder. "I've known a lot of women who worked through most of their pregnancy."

"Dangerous job for a woman."

"Firefighter's no picnic," she retorted.

"None of my girls are on the streets. One of them was, but now she works dispatch since she had a baby last year."

"That's one way," she agreed for the sake of getting along.

They finally reached her apartment and Angelo stopped the car. "Mind if I ask you a question?"

Annie shook her head. "Why am I a cop?"

"No, that's obvious to me," Angelo said, turning to face her on the seat. "Do you love my boy?"

Annie cleared her throat and felt her heartbeat triple. "I . . . uh . . ."

"No polite answers." Angelo stopped her stammering. "Do you love Tony?"

She faced him squarely. "Yes, I do."

"Good," he said, grinning at her. "That's very good. You're stubborn, but I like that. Probably means you're loyal too. I like that for Tony. He needs a good woman."

Annie had to know. "Why do you think I became a cop?"

He shrugged. "You saw your daddy going to work every day. Saw your brothers, too, and you decided you could do the job too. Even if you are a woman."

"Thanks," she said. "Thanks for the ride too. It was nice to meet you and your wife."

"It was nice to meet you too, Annie. I've worked with your father. He's a great cop."

"Good night," she said, getting out of the car.

"Good night," Angelo answered. "Don't be a stranger."

Annie had all intentions of falling into bed and not getting up again until she was due on duty. She was exhausted physically, but her brain refused to shut down and let her sleep.

In the end, after spending an hour tossing and turning, she got up, showered, drank some hot coffee, and got dressed again.

She couldn't stop thinking about how wrong she had been about Sean and his demands for her safety.

Without meaning to, she found herself parked outside his office, staring at the red brick building.

Maybe it wouldn't mean anything to him, but Annie wasn't the kind of person that liked to have things unfinished. She thought they had said all there was to say to one another. Until she realized that she had been wrong.

"Mr. Franklin will see you now," a smiling, golden-haired secretary said to her as she waited in a pastel blue-and-green lobby.

"Annie!" Sean greeted her as she crossed the threshold and entered his spacious office. He kissed her lightly and looked at her. "You're looking good. How have you been?"

"I've been good," she said, seeing him and remembering all of the good times they'd had together. "How about you?"

"I've been good too." He glanced around his office. "The business has been going well. I've been promoted a few times." He looked at her. "You're still a cop?"

She nodded. "That's why I came to see you, Sean."

He looked surprised, his handsome face showing a little trepidation. "Am I being arrested?"

"No," she assured him. "I'm not here in an official capacity. I wanted to apologize to you."

"Apologize?" he responded, puzzled. "Would you like to sit down?"

She took a seat in front of the desk while he sat behind it, staring at her.

"I wanted to apologize to you for the things I said about you being afraid about my job," she told him, not wasting any time. "I was wrong to treat your emotions that way. You had every right to feel the way you did."

Sean was clearly surprised. "What brought about this revelation?"

She shrugged, not wanting to get into that. "Let's just say that I've had an experience that made me understand what you were feeling."

"Okay," he agreed. "That must have been quite an experience to bring you all the way over here."

"It was," she told him, feeling better now that she had said what was bothering her. She stood up. "I have to go."

"Wait!" He came around the desk quickly. "Is that it? Is that all you came to say?"

She shrugged and smiled at him. "That's it."

He approached her cautiously, putting his hands on her shoulders. "What about us? We could get back together. I'm still free. I mean, I've been dating. But nothing serious. We had some good times, Annie."

"I know," she agreed with a smile after thinking the same thing.

"Then what about it? We could have dinner tonight. Eight o'clock. I could pick you up."

Annie shook her head. "I'm dating someone else, Sean. Someone serious. I just wanted you to know that I was wrong not to understand the way you felt."

He nodded and took his hands away from her shoulders. "Okay. I don't really understand. But sometimes we couldn't find a compatible wavelength. I guess that was one of our problems."

She smiled at him. "This might be one of those times."

Sean smiled and kissed her lightly on the mouth. "Good-bye, Annie. Thanks for stopping by."

Annie thought about that kiss during the ride back to the hospital, the elevator jump up to the children's floor, and while she was holding Sara, feeding her a bottle.

The baby's small hands curled around Annie's fingers and her dark eyes looked up at Annie as though she were the most special person in the whole world.

Annie had a feeling that she looked at Tony the same way. Sean's kiss had shown her how special Tony was to her.

She had already acknowledged that she loved him, but a deep feeling of tenderness, of caring, overcame her when she was with him. She wanted to be with him, to share his life.

Sara went to sleep in Annie's arms. Annie sat there for a long time, watching her sleep, thinking about what Fred and Angie had said about Tony and her adopting Sara.

They could adopt her. They could have children of their own. Dark-haired little boys and red-haired little girls. They could be a family. For the first time in a long time, she caught herself daydreaming about a man and the life they could have together. Tony Rousso with his deep, dark eyes and gentle hands.

She left Sara sleeping in her crib and walked down the halls to Tony's room, but he was already gone. The housekeeping staff stared at her as they cleaned up his room.

"They checked him out about an hour ago," the nurse told her as she passed. "He's fine. He'll be back at work letting things fall on him in no time."

Annie thanked her, thinking about the story Angelo had told her about the tree, then she got her car and headed home.

Chapter Ten

Tony was sitting on her doorstep when she got home.

"Are you all right?" she asked in amazement. "What are you doing here? Shouldn't you be home in bed?"

He frowned at her "Don't start. My mother is enough."

"Sorry," she said. "But you were hurt."

"Something came up. I tried to call," he told her when she came around the car. "I thought you were coming home to sleep."

"I couldn't sleep," she confessed, unlocking the door. "I went to see Sean."

"Sean?" Tony asked blankly as he followed her into the warm apartment. "Ex-fiancé Sean?"

166

She nodded, collapsing on the sofa. "I spent so much time thinking about him. About the things that he had said to me when we broke up. I had to see him and apologize."

Tony took the chair near the door, his injured arm cradled in a sling. "What did he say?"

She shrugged. "I think he was surprised."

"So am I," he replied.

"Why?" she demanded. "You were the one who agreed that it would be hard to live with someone who was in a dangerous job—seeing you get hurt, realizing what Sean must have felt like when I got shot. I knew I had been wrong. I wanted him to know."

Tony took off his jacket carefully, then sat back down in the chair. "Did he want to get back together with you?"

"Yes," she answered honestly, looking at him. "Want some coffee?"

"Sure," he said. "What did you say to him?"

He wondered if she could tell that he was holding his breath, waiting for her response. He watched her as she made the coffee, but her face was a tired mask.

Annie glanced up at him. "I told him that I was involved with someone else. What could I say?"

"Annie," he whispered as he pinned her against the cabinet and kissed her soundly. His mouth moved over hers and his hands stroked her back until he could feel her body relax against his and her arms crept up around his neck.

"What was that for?" she asked when she could speak.

"Being involved with someone else," he answered, breathless himself.

"Oh," she managed softly.

The coffee perked while he kissed her again. His mouth was warm and he tasted of cherry Lifesavers.

Annie gave herself up to the passion that he shared with her. Her soul was warmed by the fire she felt in his arms.

"So," she began again when he had moved away from her mouth and was following a trail that tenderly grazed her neck inside her sweater collar. "What are you doing here?"

Tony kissed her again, sweetly, on the mouth. "You won't believe what's happened."

"Something good, I hope," she ventured. "No one else got hurt, did they?"

"My uncle did last fall, but he's doing pretty well. He fell and broke his hip and had to have it replaced. He's going to need to live closer in to the city to be near his doctors and therapy. That's where my luck comes in."

Tony poured them both a cup of coffee. Annie added cream and sugar. Then they returned to the other room.

She could tell he was excited about something and wanted to tell her in the right setting.

"So, he wants to trade. My house for his dairy farm." Tony continued his explanation when they were sitting down again. "It's a working farm. He's got about a hundred head of milk cows and a few stores that he already sells to on a regular basis. It won't be an even trade, but the payments will be reasonable and short term.''

Annie looked at him. Had she missed something? ''What are you saying?''

''That the dream can come true. I told you how I felt about living someplace out of the city, like Angie and Fred. It's real now. It can happen.''

She took a sip of her coffee and digested his information. ''So, you're going to move, give up your career with the department, and raise cows?''

Tony frowned. Her assessment of his dream sounded less than wonderful. There was no excitement on her face or in her voice when he shared his news.

He decided to try another tack. ''Remember how we felt that Fred and Angie's farm would be a great place to raise Sara? She wouldn't have to live with them to get that now, Annie.''

''I don't know what to say,'' she finally stated, looking at his excited, glowing eyes and wide grin. She took a worried sip of her coffee.

While it was true that he had mentioned that he wanted a farm and wanted to live outside the city, she hadn't believed that he was ever really planning on doing it.

''You don't like the idea?''

She smiled uncertainly at him. ''I'm a city girl, Tony. I've never had an aunt or anyone that lived outside the city. I understand that this is your dream, but . . .''

Tony put down his cup of coffee and came to sit beside her on the sofa. He took her coffee as well and set it down, then took her hand in his.

"Maybe I'm not doing this the right way. Annie, I'd like you to marry me. Come with me to the dairy farm. We could adopt Sara and raise her ourselves. We could have a great life together.''

Annie looked into his dark eyes and words failed her. Part of it was the words she wanted to hear. Part of it left her gasping for breath.

"What about the rest of your family, Tony? Your parents and brothers and sisters. You're all very close. How will they take this?''

Tony shrugged, stung by her less than enthusiastic reception of his proposal. It wasn't going the way he had envisioned when he had spoken to his uncle.

"They get free milk. They've always been close to my grandparents and my uncle when he inherited the farm. There's no reason to think that fifty miles outside the city is going to make us strangers.''

"I don't know if my family has ever driven that far outside the city,'' she said with a small smile. But she didn't look up at him. "I was going to take the test to make detective first class next month. The first ever in my family to get out of a uniform.''

Tony paused. Was there something that he was missing about their relationship that was making this impossible? Did she just not want to marry him and couldn't figure out a better way to tell him?

"I know your career is important to you," he began, exercising more restraint than he had ever found before in his life. "I know you and Sean parted ways over him asking you to give up your job, but this is different."

Annie stared at him. "How is you finding your dream but asking me to give up mine different?"

Tony sat up straight and let go of her hands. "Is that what I'm asking you to do? Give up your dream to find mine?"

"That's what it seems like to me."

"What about love, Annie? Do you love me?"

She could feel the tension in him, feel him slipping away from her, but if she went with him, everything she had ever known would be gone. Everything she had ever wanted would be here in the city and she would be on a dairy farm. What could she say?

"I do love you, Tony, but—"

"But not enough to give up your dream," he finished her statement. "You shouldn't. No one should love someone else more than they love their dream."

"If I asked you to stay here and give up your dream because you loved me, what would you say?" she demanded, close to tears.

"Try it," he said fiercely. "Try asking me if I love you and if I would go anywhere or do anything to be with you."

He stared at her, daring her to make any overture, but she didn't reply. She looked at her hands, which were curled in her lap.

"Are you afraid that I might stay? That I might

love you enough to give up anything to be with you?''

''No,'' she denied, lifting her head to look at him as he stood up from the sofa. ''I wouldn't ask that of you. I wouldn't ask that of anyone. This is your dream. You should have it.''

Tony walked to the chair where he'd left his coat with wooden strides. ''I thought this was the best day of my life. The day I could offer you a new life. A life with Sara and with me. I guess I was wrong.''

''Tony!'' she called out as he walked to the door.

He turned back to face her, his face a mask trying to hide the pain he was feeling.

''Do you love me?''

He stared at her, unseeing. ''What difference does it make?''

Annie cried herself to sleep after Tony left her. She woke up that afternoon with a pounding headache and her eyes almost swollen shut. Before she did anything else, she took two aspirin and put a cold cloth over her eyes.

Why had this happened? She knew plenty of people who married, had similar dreams, lived similar lives. First she had Sean, who couldn't handle it when she had been shot. Then there was Tony whose dream was to leave everything behind and brave a whole new world.

Maybe she needed to date another officer, she considered miserably. Maybe she just needed to give up dating altogether. Maybe she would never, never fall in love with anyone again. Life was hard enough. Why inflict this pain on herself?

As soon as she felt that she could face the world, she showered and dressed warmly. She wore makeup to help camouflage the fact that she had been crying, but she wasn't sure it worked. She was miserable and she looked it.

She had decided to visit Sara at the hospital. It might be for the last time. Holding the baby they had saved together sounded more depressing than anything else she could imagine, but she knew there was solace in those little arms as well.

She wanted to cry until she couldn't find any tears left in her. She wanted to hide away from everyone and everything and hope that no one came looking for her. But she was too practical to do any of those things. Problems were meant to be faced head-on. No compromise, no quarter.

She wrapped a red scarf around her neck and buttoned her jacket against the cold. She was going to face the world.

She saw him the moment she walked into the nursery. It was like a deliberate slap in the face. She stopped cold, as though her feet were frozen in the doorway.

He was sitting in the chair, holding Sara and tickling her feet. She was laughing and clapping her hands, making burbling sounds at him as he talked to her.

Annie watched them for a few minutes. He was as in love with Sara as she was and losing her was going to be hard for him as well. Was that why he had come up with the plan to move to the farm? Was he saving Sara from any other unhappiness?

It had to be more than that, she decided. Though he obviously cared for the baby, she didn't believe he was giving up his career and his life just for her. This was something he had really wanted to do. His dream, as he had called it. He wanted to escape the city to live on the land. Fresh air and blue skies.

Why couldn't it be her dream as well? she wondered. Was it so much to ask when her whole body felt as though she had been beaten? When all of her heart and soul was crying to go with him and forget everything else?

She closed her eyes and wished that it could have been different. She wished that he was holding a child of their own on his lap and she had been watching him from the kitchen door. She wished that there could be a compromise between his dream and hers.

It didn't seem so much, really, just a place between the farm, and living in the city doing the work she loved. But if it existed, it eluded her.

Instead, he would be moving to his farm and she would be going on with her life. Sara would be happy with Angie and Fred. Everything would be as it was supposed to be.

Everything except your broken heart, a small voice inside of her whispered. *Everything except you being miserable for the rest of your life.*

She didn't recall hurting so much when she had decided that she and Sean had no future together. She had been unhappy, but it hadn't felt as though the rest of her life was over. How could she stay and live her dream if her heart was somewhere with Tony on his dairy farm?

"Excuse me," a nurse said, passing her to enter the nursery.

Tony turned and Annie looked at him, trying to keep her feelings out of her eyes.

"Hi," she said breezily. "How's Sara?"

"She's fine," he answered, looking away from her quickly. "The nurse said she's gained five pounds since she came here. She just needed some attention."

"What everyone needs," she murmured, standing near his shoulder and looking into the baby's face.

Sara reached her little arms out for Annie to take her and Tony relinquished the baby to her.

"Have you heard anything about her parents?" he asked her.

Annie shook her head. "They couldn't find any record of her being born. The mother probably had her outside of the hospital. Maybe a teenager who can't come forward and claim her. They don't expect the case to ever be solved."

Tony touched the baby's downy soft head and Sara grabbed his hand. "She'll have a good life, anyway, with Angie and Fred."

"She will," Annie agreed, her heart already aching with the sure knowledge that Sara would be gone.

Tony looked at her as though he wanted to say

something more. Then he looked at his watch instead and muttered about the time.

"Are you still working?" Annie asked.

He nodded. "I've put in my notice. It will take the two weeks to pack and move anyway. Probably take longer for my uncle to get rid of his stuff and clear out of the house."

"That sounds great," she told him, trying to look at him without crying. "I hope everything goes well for you."

"Thanks," he replied naturally, although his voice sounded strained to his own ears.

He wanted to kiss her until she couldn't breathe. He wanted to make her forget Sean and not care whether she lived in the city or the country, as long as she was with him.

Instead, he smiled and left her there with the baby. *Their* baby. Sara could have been their own. They could have been her parents instead of Fred and Angie.

He walked out into the watery sunlight and wondered what was wrong with the world. He had never loved anyone the way he loved Annie. Why couldn't she feel the same about him?

Annie nuzzled her nose into Sara's sweet-smelling neck to disguise the tears that were running down her cheeks. It could have been so different. Why did everything always fall apart?

Annie stood watching at the side of Sara's crib after she was asleep for a long time. Sara wasn't her baby, she told herself. Someday, she would meet the right person and she would have children of her own. But she would never forget Sara. She would never forget Tony.

Depressed by the unexpected turn of events, Annie went to visit her mother. She sat in her warm kitchen drinking chamomile tea and eating fresh strawberry tarts.

Maybe she would move back home. It would be nice to have people around her for a while. She didn't think her parents would object. With all of her brothers and sisters gone, the house was more than half empty.

With a new batch of tarts in the oven, her mother sat down at the table with her youngest daughter.

"So what's the problem?" she asked pointedly.

Annie mumbled, denying that there was a problem.

Her mother refused to believe it. "Not that I'm not flattered that you just wanted to come and spend time with me, but I can tell by the makeup on your face that something's wrong. You've been crying." She stared at her daughter. "It's him, isn't it?"

"Him?" Annie asked, clearing her throat.

"Tony Rousso, the fireman. Did you have a fight?"

"He's moving away," Annie told her with a sniff.

"Moving away where?" her mother asked.

Annie explained the circumstances. Her mother listened and nodded.

"So, you don't want to live on a dairy farm and he has his heart set on it?"

"He said I shouldn't give up my dream of being

a detective for his dream, no matter how much I love him. He told me to ask him to give up his dream for me, but I couldn't . . . I couldn't.''

Katie O'Malley studied her daughter as she was miserably eating tarts and sipping tea. ''Ask him.''

''Ask him?''

''Ask him to stay in the city. Ask him to stay with you. People have made greater sacrifices.''

Annie balked. ''How could I look at him every day for the rest of our lives? He wouldn't love me at all, if he loves me now.''

''What are we talking about, Annie? Didn't he say that he loves you?'' her mother asked.

''He asked me to marry him. He said we could adopt Sara and raise her on the farm. But he didn't say he loved me.''

''Did you ask him?'' her mother wondered, holding her breath, praying as she did every day to see her daughter in white lace.

''I did,'' Annie replied softly. ''He said it didn't matter.''

''Do you love him?''

''I do love him,'' Annie muttered unhappily. ''I don't think he loves me.''

''But you don't know for sure, do you? Talk to him, Annie. Maybe there's a compromise to be found on your dreams. Maybe you can both have something you love without hating each other. If he wants to marry you, he must love you.''

Annie swallowed the rest of her tart. Maybe her

mother was right. Maybe she should talk to him about it.

She watched her mother take another tray of tarts from the oven. "How do you live with it?"

"With what?" her mother wondered.

"Knowing that Dad could be hurt or killed every time he goes out on the job."

"I don't think about it much," she answered. "And when it does come up, I pray. That's how I live with it."

"I never really understood until Tony was hurt. I thought about it with Dad and Patrick and everyone else in the family, but it never really hit home until Tony was hurt."

Her mother smiled at her. "Good. Does that mean you'll give up the force now?"

Annie smiled. "If I go and live on Tony's farm, I suppose I'll have to."

"Will you be happy doing that, Annie? This is all you've ever wanted since you were a little girl. Can you give up everything to make Tony, or me, happy?"

Annie considered her mother's words. She did love Tony, but living on the farm with him would mean giving up her career. She had survived five years on the streets and was about to take her test to become a detective. Did she want another life?

"I don't know."

"You'd better think about that before you talk to Tony. Be sure what you want, Annie."

"Thanks, Mom." Annie hugged her impulsively.

She took another tart with her. "I'll let you know what happens."

Katie O'Malley sighed as she watched her daughter walk out the door.

Angelo Rousso was waiting outside of her apartment. His huge old car was blowing dark smoke into the frosty air.

"Mr. Rousso?" she called as she got out of her car.

He opened the window and smiled at her. "You've broken my son's heart."

"Mr. Rousso—"

"Angelo, please," he told her. "Didn't you tell me that you loved Tony?"

She nodded miserably. "I do love Tony. It just seems like we can't live together."

"What do you mean?" he demanded. "What kind of thing is that to say?"

"I don't know," Annie admitted. "Where is Tony?"

"He drove out to the farm to help his uncle."

"Can you give me directions?" she asked.

"I knew it would work out for the two of you," he responded, waving a piece of paper with a carefully drawn map. "Love is wonderful!"

Annie wasn't so sure, but she felt like she had to give it one more try. She didn't want to lose Tony, even if it meant giving up her own dream. She had to talk to him, make him understand.

The drive out from the city wasn't as bad as she

had imagined. The roads were clear and traffic was light.

Maybe it wouldn't be so bad, she considered, watching as the city landscape changed to the flat, rolling countryside. She wouldn't be that far from her family. They could visit each other.

As for her career in law enforcement, while it was true that she had always wanted to follow in her father's footsteps, she knew that she wanted to be with Tony more. It had been a surprise when he had first told her about the farm. She just had to have a chance to think about it.

That was the way she planned on presenting it to Tony, if he would listen. She had needed time to get used to the idea. She wanted to live with Tony, and possibly little Sara, anywhere that made him happy. She could be happy there as well.

It was starting to get dark when she came to the sleepy little town of Mayfield. The farm was just outside the town limits. There were a few stores still open on the main street. A small hotel, a feed store, and a bus station made up the rest of the town.

Looking at Angelo's instructions, she noticed that there wasn't a road where the map said there should have been. Spotting the sheriff's station at the edge of Mayfield, she pulled in the parking lot and walked inside.

An hour later, she walked back out, climbed back into her car and sat, unmoving, while she considered what had just happened to her.

More than directions to the Rousso dairy, Annie

found herself with a new job. When she had told the sheriff that she was an officer in Chicago, he had offered her the job of lead deputy without hesitation. The salary was good and the career possibilities were different than she had expected, but not without merit.

She looked at the badge in her hand. Was this the compromise she had been looking for? They could live on Tony's farm and she could still have her career. It seemed to be the perfect answer.

Disregarding all speed limit signs, she left Mayfield behind and headed for the dairy farm. Her heart was light and her mind was soaring ahead to the future they could have together. Anything was possible, she decided, feeling the deputy's badge in her pocket again just to be sure it had really happened. It could work. They could both have their dreams.

The Rousso farm was bigger than she had anticipated. It sprawled out over a hundred acres with several freshly painted barns and a huge white house standing on a hill.

It was like a scene from a child's book, she thought, looking at it as she drove up the tree-lined driveway. Golden light spilled out from the windows of the house. Black and white cows were being led into their stalls for the night. A sliver of a new moon was coming up on the horizon.

Annie could understand Tony's attachment for the place. It looked like a wonderful place to raise children and spend long evenings in front of the fire. A perfect place for Sara.

Hopefully, she sighed, getting out of the car, a perfect place for love.

She knocked on the door, then waited, shivering in the cold wind. Her heart in her throat, she tried to think of what she would say when she saw Tony's face. Her mind was blank.

The door opened, yellow light spilling out on the dark front porch illuminating an old swing and rocking chair.

"Annie?"

"Tony?"

He stared at her for a long minute, as though he couldn't believe that she was there in front of him.

The light from inside was behind him so that she couldn't see his face. What was he thinking?

"I'm sorry. Come on in," he said finally, as though he had just realized that he had been staring at her.

"Thanks."

He closed the door behind her but didn't make any move to lead her through the dark front room to the well-lighted kitchen she could see down the hall.

"What are you doing here?" he wondered.

She looked up at him. "I . . . I couldn't let you go."

He didn't say another word. His arms folded around her and drew her close to him. His head rested on hers as he held her. She could hear his heart beat, strong and real in her ear.

"It does matter," he whispered at last. "I do love you, Annie."

"I love you," she answered, shaking with cold and the strength of her emotions.

He kissed her. The exquisite agony of nearly breaking up made it sweeter. It pierced her to the heart as she clung to him and hoped he would never let her go.

"I've been explaining to my uncle that I can't take the farm," he told her when they had managed to move a centimeter apart from each other. "It was my dream to live here, but you're my dream now. I don't want to live anywhere without you. And I don't want you to give up your dream."

Annie felt hot, silent tears sliding down her face. "I came to tell you the same thing. I would rather live out here with you than have any career."

"I don't have the right to take that away from you," he said, kissing the side of her face gently, tasting her tears on his lips. He vowed that he would never make her cry again.

She sniffed and wiped away the tears, smiling at him in the dim light. "Well, as it happens, I already have a new job."

"What?" he wondered.

She took the deputy's badge out of her pocket. "I was coming to tell you that we could find some compromise, even if I had to give up my job or I had to talk you into staying in Chicago. Instead, I found the perfect middle road. I'm Mayfield's newest deputy. Maybe someday, I'll be sheriff."

He stared at her without speaking. Then he kissed her so hard that it took her breath away.

"Are you sure?" he asked.

"It'll still be a dangerous job," she reminded him.

He laughed. "But I'll have the most beautiful deputy in Mayfield in my arms every night."

She sighed. "That you will since I'm the first female deputy in Mayfield. And we can find out about adopting Sara ourselves."

He kissed her ear. "Then we can see about making a few babies together."

"Mmmm."